Unforgiven in
CHESHIRE BAY

USA TODAY BESTSELLING AUTHOR
H.M. SHANDER

Other Books by H.M. Shander

Duly Noted – book 1
That Summer – book 2
If You Say Yes – book 3
Serving Up Innocence
Serving Up Devotion
Serving Up Secrecy
Serving Up Hope
It All Began with a Note
It All Began with a Mai-Tai
It All Began with a Wedding
Noel
Whistler's Night
Behind the Mask
Return to Cheshire Bay
Adrift in Cheshire Bay
Awake in Cheshire Bay
Christmas in Cheshire Bay
Journey to Cheshire Bay
Charmed in Cheshire Bay
Second Chances in Cheshire Bay
Unforgiven in Cheshire Bay
Flirty in Cheshire Bay

Up to Date listings can be found on the website:
www.hmshander.com

Table of Contents

Chapter One

This was it. The big reveal. One of the custom pieces I'd designed and put my blood, sweat, and tears into. The blood, thankfully, didn't actually make it onto the carving, but there was a stain on the floor of my workshop I'd forever remember as the Stain of Tarkin.

The Bayside Market was bustling, and thanks to an unseasonably warmer than average August, the place was packed. I hadn't had a chance to sit and work all day on the piece I'd brought with me, but that was okay. I was selling out of my smaller pieces and getting ready to unveil a custom order for a new friend. I'd taken some of my friend Libby's ideas, and covered the piece with a tablecloth, setting it in front of my table, waiting, almost impatiently, for Dr. Chloe Tarkin to arrive for the grand unveiling.

As she arrived, I stood like a Price is Right model, hand on top of the edge of the frame, a giant smile on my face, and my other hand on my ample hip.

"Oh my god, Erin, is that it?" Chloe's voice pierced through the crowd as the bubbly blonde pushed her way over to my table.

"It sure is."

I waited to yank it off. A crowd was gathering, much to my delight. Hopefully, if the customers saw the work, they would be interested in ordering their own custom design, and if not, I always had a few carvings on my table ready for immediate sale. Either way, this was a helpful boost to my shaken confidence.

Dr. Tarkin stood ready. Hands folded together, she kept tapping them against her lips. Like me, she loved the excitement building, I could see it in her eyes.

"Are you ready?" I asked, cocking an eyebrow.

My hands twitched in excitement as I gripped a bit of the red tablecloth and teased the bottom of the artwork.

She squealed with delight and grabbed her boyfriend's hand. "Oh my god, I can't wait."

BJ Sutcliff, a local author, twisted away and whispered something in her ear, and she blushed slightly as she playfully bumped into his chest.

"Unveil it already. I'm going crazy." Her eyes widened.

"Here we go." I ripped off the red fabric and sent it flying behind my table display.

Propped up against the front of the table was her custom piece – a four-by-three-foot wooden frame, with intricately carved trees, stacked in five lines to give a sense of depth to the woodwork. Born from a sketched idea, I made a prototype and photographed it. Naturally, that was the single piece Dr. Tarkin fell in love with when she perused my brag book.

"You like it?" I surveyed her wide eyes and generous smile. She positively glowed, but then again, I could never really tell if the person was being genuine or putting on a good show.

"I freaking love it." She hunched down to touch it gingerly as if it would break.

Sweet relief sighed out of me, and I smiled in appreciation.

"I used the actual types of trees for each row; Douglas Fir, Weeping Willow, Red Cedar, Common Beech, and at the back is White Pine." I touched each row as I mentioned the wood grain by name. "It's all edged in the Douglas Fir, which is a little unorthodox, but I wanted it to look like this first row of trees were growing right off the frame."

"It's amazing." She went to lift it and must've been prepared for a solid weight as she nearly launched it into the air.

"Trade secret."

Not too long ago I figured out how to hollow out the wood without losing strength, so my chisel didn't go right on through and crack a work of art. It was a huge learning curve, but the end result was fantastic – it wasn't heavy, and any hanging artwork wouldn't pull its hanger down the wall.

A taller man, with broad shoulders like a linebacker, pushed through the crowd and stopped in front of Dr. Tarkin's paid artwork.

"Wow, that is some piece. I've been searching for something unique and jaw-dropping to have at work, and this is exactly what I need." He popped his head up and looked down at me. "I'll take it right now. How much?"

Dr. Tarkin didn't look too impressed and quickly wrapped her hands around the artwork.

Her boyfriend stepped closer to her. "Should I load it up in the car?"

"But I was interested in it first."

Omg, is the cute guy actually whining?

"It's already been sold." Dr. Tarkin cleared her throat. "It was a custom piece I ordered from Erin here."

The linebacker pulled down on his beard and twisted in my direction. "Really? Custom ordered, eh?"

I crossed my finger over my chest. "Honest to God truth. I made it myself."

"I'm good to take this, Erin?" Chloe – Dr. Tarkin – stood ready to go.

"You bet. It's ready to hang." Walking around to the back of my display, I grabbed the waiting envelope I had and handed it over. "Your receipt is tucked inside, and there are mounting instructions as well. A paper fold-out to place on your wall that will match up with the holders."

"Wow, you thought of everything. Thank you."

I beamed. A happy customer was a great gift since they told

their friends and families, and word travelled by mouth. That was the best kind of advertising, and I couldn't pay for that. Trust me, I'd tried.

Putting on my friendliest smile, I thanked her for choosing Erin's Woodworking, but it wasn't catchy like some of the other names in the Cheshire Bay town. Using my personal name was boring in comparison, however, having my woodworking pay the bills was a new one for me. So much better than waitressing and whatever odd job I could find. Wood carving was my passion, and it allowed me to be home with my daughter, aside from market days when she hung out with my energetic younger sister and did fun aunty-niece activities.

I turned my attention back to the handsome guy standing in front of my table. There was an assessing expression chiseled onto his face, and it didn't seem like it was my work he was checking out. As the slight possibility of it being me he was judging, my heart beat a little bit faster.

"So, how can I help you, Sir?"

He was older than me, maybe mid to late thirties, perhaps even beyond that. No signs of greying temples, but there was a certain wisdom to the wrinkles around his eyes that alluded to not being so fresh off the farm, something we likely had in common.

"I really liked that piece. Can you make another like it?" There was a twinkle to the browns of his eyes, which were like a fresh coat of polish over a mahogany stain. They were mesmerizing.

"I would be very happy to custom design something similar for you." I wrapped my hands around the edge of the table, tapping a finger underneath in an effort to control my suddenly rapid breathing. "Were you thinking trees on the horizon? Or would there be something different I can create?"

"You really do custom?" He leaned a little closer, bridging the already narrow distance between us.

"All the time. If you tell me a little about the space you're looking for, I can throw out some ideas." For good measure, I put my brag book front and centre of the table, and opened to the first page. "These are the carvings I've done." I rifled through the page-protected photos with my unadorned left hand, as if to show him I wasn't attached. At all. "And after this tab, these are some of the ideas I'm sketching out to recreate in my workshop."

"She's amazing and uber-talented." Libby, a trusted friend, piped up like she always did, while she leaned on her own table next to mine. "Have you ever seen her work?"

"Just that last piece." His focus bounced from the brag book to Libby – who always managed to catch everyone's eyes with her short skirt and thigh-high stockings, with beautiful blonde hair in two long braids; the ends which looked like they'd been dipped in ink and spread up half the length of her hair – and back over to plain-Jane me.

My gaze settled like a fog on the ocean, making everything just a little bit fuzzy.

My friend cleared her throat. "Well, you should check out Pita Pete's. He's got a whale tail on display near the register. Incredible detail. And the Knitter's Knot sells the bowls that she can't keep in stock here." Libby looked the man up and down. "But I don't think you're a knitting kind of guy."

He chuckled, a low throaty melodic sound; one I could listen to forever if given the chance. Cute guy never removed his connection from me, all the while running his fingers through his thick, dark hair. "No, can't say that I am."

"Well," Libby carried on, pointing to the carvings on display. "She also has these smaller pieces available. Perfect for a desk or workspace."

Who needed a marketer? Libby was a fantastic salesperson, and she didn't even focus solely on her own items. Seriously, she could sell wool to a sheep farmer and convince him what she was selling was far superior to his own.

"I'll take a look, thanks."

The guy picked up a smaller whale tail carving on my table. It was the perfect souvenir as whale watching season was in full swing, and I typically had none left by the end of the market. He ran a finger over the markings on the tail. Each was unique, just like the whales in the real were.

"You do this yourself? Is it a family business?"

I forced myself to tear my gaze away from his intensity. Was he interested in what I was selling, or was it more? More often than not, guys did a quick look and moved on, preferring the infectious bubbly nature Libby had in spades, and yet with this guy, it was different.

Bobbing my head in response to his question, I swallowed before answering. "No, just me. Sole proprietor and owner and long-term employee." I shook my head. He didn't need to know that. "But the carving doesn't take me too long. I find it quite soothing to work the wood into what I vision."

"And this is all you have left?"

The table was half full of smaller pieces as, lucky for me, I'd sold out of the larger pieces I'd worked on all week. Tourists were a gold mine and hit the market early to cherry-pick everyone's tables. I loved it.

"Fraid so." I pointed to the book again, a natural smile bubbling to my lips as I glanced up at him. "But, seriously, I'm happy to make you anything you'd like in the book."

"And if I wanted a full wall mural, or a giant artwork?"

"That can totally be arranged." I swallowed down a buildup of excitement and kept my toe tapping to a minimum. What he was talking about would be bank for me. Desperately needed bank.

I tucked a strand of my dark, wavy hair behind my ear, and broke eye contact with him.

It was intense, and just a little ridiculous at how it fired up my long dormant butterflies. Plain crazy, if you'd asked me. Guys like him never stuck around with me. I had too much baggage for them.

After catching him staring at me, I pushed down the flurry of flutters and flipped to a sample contract I kept in the far back of the brag book, behind another tab. "Just for full disclosure, I will do a quick, free consultation, however, once I start drawing up plans, I require a 50% non-refundable deposit."

"Sounds fair."

"Good." I smiled, my heart hammering like a teenager.

Some customers had balked at paying a deposit, but there were no guarantees they'd pay for the work once completed. At least this way, I got something out of it and with any luck, I could sell the project at a later date if they changed their mind, which had yet to happen. Thankfully.

"I'm doing some much-needed renovations, and I think a centerpiece like this would be great. Plus, it has all that buy-local appeal." He paused and gazed upon me thoughtfully. "You are local, correct?"

"Yes. I live in Cheshire Bay."

"Perfect. I'm just across the inlet." There was a warmth in his perfect grin, along with his non-threatening stance, that suddenly put me at ease. "Let's schedule a consultation, if that's okay?"

"I'd like that."

He reached into his back pocket, and retrieved a brown leather wallet, the same colour as the wood I'd just stained yesterday; a dark walnut. From it, he pulled out a business card. "My number's on the bottom."

Thumbing my personal stack of plain Jane business cards, which held nothing more than *Erin's Eclectic Woodshop*, and my number, he picked one up and gave it a quick tap against his finger. "Just in case you lose my card, I have a way to reach you." He glanced at the card. "Erin, I assume?"

"Yes, and thank you." Preferring not to look at the moment, I tucked his card into my apron. "I'll call you on Monday to set something up."

"I look forward to it." With a charming wink that heated me more than I ever thought possible, he waved quickly and disappeared into the bustling crowd.

"Well, well, well." Libby clucked beside me. "You looked like you were ready to mount that guy right here and now."

"What?" My eyes bugged out. "I so was not."

I hadn't had the faintest heat cross my cheeks, and I hadn't battled my eyes like some ridiculous teenager. My butterflies had been invisible, so I wasn't sure what Libby saw.

"You were." She handed her customer a bag of freshly baked goodies. "But it's all good. Another custom piece would be a gold mine for you."

"It really would. It would help pay off the mounting medical bills. That shit isn't cheap."

My daughter's bills were starting to creep higher and higher, not all specialists were covered under health care, and the devices she needed were exponentially higher with each upgrade. And those upgrades were happening faster than originally predicted.

The regular wood pieces I created were my bread and gravy, and I was able to use those to pay the bills, but it would be nice to have the custom work provide a bit of cushion; a luxury I'd never had.

People mingled in front of my table, and a customer purchased a whale tail, after sharing her tale about a whale-watching expedition she'd recently been on. These were my biggest sellers, mostly because it was prime whale watching season, and at the other end of the market, there was a guy with a tour company pitching his services. I really ought to have collaborated with him – put his business cards at my table, in exchange for having one of my whale tails at his booth. It could still be done. There were a couple months left to the market – assuming the favourable weather we'd been having held out into Thanksgiving.

As ideas and images sprang to my head over what kind of piece I could create for the noteworthy guy I'd be calling on Monday, I realized I never got his name. Pulling out his card, I stared bug-eyed at the logo, with his name *David Dean* written above the word *owner*.

So that's what the son-of-a-bitch looks like.

Never met the devil in person, but I knew that name, and far worse, I knew that place. And there was no way in hell I was doing business with him. Not after what he had done.

Chapter Two

Crumpling the card in my palm, I shoved it into the bottom of my apron's pocket and sat down on my stool, ignoring the customers perusing the art pieces. With my gouging tool in hand, I urged it through a thick piece of wood.

Libby danced over and came to a full stop beside me. "Erin, you're as white as a ghost."

I blinked away the darkness, shaking my head as I stared at the crooked line I'd just carved, wondering how I was going to salvage this. "Damn. Sorry. I just… A thought, a memory…"

It had all come rushing back with the sight of the business name, and like the undertow in the ocean, threatened to pull me under just as quickly.

"How are your sales?" I needed the distraction her upbeat voice provided.

"Well, Sylvia's going to be thrilled as always. Do you want

anything before it's all gone?" She stood a few feet away with her hands on her hips and tipped her double-braided head to the side. Although she was younger than me by a dozen years at least, she gave me a motherly look.

"I'm fine. I'm just not sure I want to do business with that guy."

"That cute one? The one who wants a huge centerpiece?"

"That's the guy."

"Why on earth not?" She held up a nibbled fingertip in a one-second pose and leapt back to assist the customer.

I surveyed the crowd, watching as the people mingled about, with the occasional person lifting and admiring my work. They liked to watch my handiwork as well, so I pushed the gouger through the wood.

Sometimes I let the work show itself, and most of the time, it became something beautiful. Other times, I had to force it and manipulate it into what I knew it could be – and those pieces, they were usually the last ones to be purchased. Go figure.

Putting on my serious, dedicated expression of furrowed brows and rolling my shoulders forward, I pushed the tool through the chunk of red cedar wood and picked up the spoon knife to carve things out. Yep, this had all the makings of a little bunny, especially as his long ears came into shape.

Libby popped back over to my table, standing still, yet keeping an eye on things. "So why can't you commission a piece for

Mr. Tall and Good-looking?"

"Because years ago he screwed me over." My focus stayed firmly locked onto the wood.

"What? How?"

I turned the bunny to face the opposite direction and with one gentle push, the ear popped out nicely, and with my spoon knife, I hollowed out his inner ear.

"Nicely done." Libby hunkered down to meet me eye-to-eye. "But you're ignoring my question."

I sighed and put the tools on the leather holder. "When I was pregnant with Vera, I ate at his little restaurant, and I got food poisoning."

Standing, she shrugged. "Big deal."

"You're right, normally, not a huge deal at all. For most. However, I became so violently ill, like for days, and I missed work. I'd called in sick, but because I'd missed too many shifts, they let me go."

She scrunched up her face. "I don't think they can do that. Sounds like a human rights violation or something."

"That place, The Blue Fish diner, they weren't exactly on the up and up to begin with. They paid me in cash each week, and I can't say for certain, since they never provided me with tax documentation, but I assume I wasn't actually on payroll."

At least, these were things I figured out not too long ago, not almost seven years ago when I was pregnant and desperate for any kind of job to pay the bills.

"Where is this place?"

Heart hammering from the vivid memory, I channeled that energy into carving out a back leg on my bunny. "No surprise, they've since shut down, but they were not too far from here in Stewart Surf."

"Sucky." She hopped back over to her table to serve another customer.

A lady in front of my table stopped and checked out the items. "You make all these?"

"Every single one." I beamed and wiped my hands on the towel I'd set on my lap, rising to a standing position.

"Wow." She fingered the last whale tail I had, one stained in a shade of espresso. "I just went on a tour."

"Did you see anything?"

Apparently, it depended on the company, so I heard. One made sure they saw *something* whereas a couple of others were more than happy to take the money, and hope for the best, but it really was a matter of luck on Mother Nature's part to have them swim on by.

She lit up like a plugged-in Christmas tree. "We did. A whole pod of them."

"That's a fantastic memory. Did it look like this?" Gently, I ran my finger across the trailing edge of the fluke.

"We saw grey whales. Is that a grey whale?"

Honestly, I didn't know and hoped she wasn't a marine

biologist or something. "Yes, it is."

Her eyes widened in excitement, and she flipped it over to inspect the price tag. "Oh."

"It takes me a couple of hours to make and sand each one, plus the cost of materials."

"Oh, I know. Arts and crafts items never make back the effort and time put into them. It's such a shame. I think you'd sell more if you priced these cheaper." She set the piece down and offered me a smile.

I wanted to glare, but instead, I twisted my grin from genuine to plastered. "I know, it's so hard. We still have bills to pay, and kids to feed, and if I priced them any lower, I'd be giving them away."

Her expression morphed into a curious one. Was she expecting me to actually give it to her for free?

"You know what, I should probably raise the price on that one, since it's my last one. This morning I started with a dozen, and they sold out fast. Maybe I'm actually underpricing them?"

That knocked the wind out of her sails, and she stared blankly.

I challenged her, leaning forward, ready to pounce should she have another backhanded comment about the arts and craft industry. If we charged minimum wage for our time, plus the cost of materials, every piece would be at least double, and most likely, I wouldn't sell out. Pricing them the way I did, at least afforded me a marginal income.

"Well, good luck to you." Without accepting my test, she walked away.

Libby's head tilted back in full laughter. "There's one in every crowd, isn't there?"

I shook my head, feeling another wavy strand free itself from its hold. Damn hot, humid weather, and crookedly curly hair.

"So, you got fired from your job? Because you were sick?" Interestingly, Libby jumped right back into the conversation we'd had a few minutes ago. I'd hoped she'd forgotten.

How she was able to pick up like there hadn't been a break was staggering. I'd often forget where I set my tools, let alone where exactly in a conversation I was.

"Uh, right. Yeah, I lost my job." Seeing how the crowds in my area were starting to thin out, I sat back to carve. "I was scrambling to pay rent, as I lived paycheck to shitty paycheck, and was coming up empty. I contacted the restaurant where I got the food poisoning and asked if there was a way to compensate me. I didn't want millions, just what I'd lost in wages, we're talking maybe a couple hundred bucks. Enough to make up the shortfall in my rent."

"And he didn't?" She popped out her hip and firmly placed her hand on it.

"Not only did he not offer me a *thing,* he actually laughed at me and told me I was out to lunch because I had zero proof I got sick at his restaurant." I shook my head, and disgust sprang a leak in my words. "As I explained how I was pregnant and had lost my job because I'd been in the hospital, he hung up on me."

"He what?"

"Yeah, customer service wasn't his strong suit." I dug a little harder and deeper into my block of wood, making the foot come alive.

"So you lost your job, pregnant I may add, and he wouldn't even cover a little bit in rent? Like nothing? He couldn't even give you something like a free meal?"

I shook my head.

"Fucking jerk."

A mother walking by covered her child's ears and shot daggers at Libby, who shrugged.

I laughed. My daughter, who was about that age, likely knew the proper usage of the f-word, all in part to Libby's astonishing use of it. It's not like my kid was never going to hear it, just as long as she didn't use the grown-up word. I refused to shelter her too much. She had bigger issues to deal with than profanity.

"After that, I vowed I would never eat in his establishment." Among other things.

"And?"

"Oh, I've kept my word." And tried to make sure others didn't eat there either. But that wasn't as successful as I'd dreamed, since there was always a long wait for seats on the weekends and the small-town people were often commenting on the place.

"Good for you." Libby nodded in approval. "So, I take it,

you're not going to commission a piece for him."

"Absolutely not. He can go to hell."

Libby shifted on her feet; she refused to stand still. She tapped her finger against her lips. "But your custom pieces are your big-ticket items, right?"

"Yeah." I narrowed my eyes. What was she thinking?

"And you make bank with them?"

"Pretty damn close. They help cover additional expenses that always seem to surface."

Like the water heater last month. And the bald tires on my truck a couple months back – although to be fair, I only purchased take-offs, a slightly used set from another vehicle.

"So why don't you accept his offer, and make something unique for him?"

"I don't want my name associated with his business."

She rocked back and forth, her head tipped up to the roof of the tent. "But, and hear me out, he doesn't know the true cost, right?"

"No. The custom prices aren't listed anywhere, that's what the consult is for."

"For his piece, raise the cost. Tack on the pain and suffering, all your lost wages, everything he screwed you over for. Add it into his bill, somehow, somewhere. You're smart, you could figure out how."

"No, I can't. I can't just add a pain and suffering surcharge, like a shipping and handling charge." No doubt if he saw that on the bill, he'd refuse. I certainly would. And I'd blackball the person who did it to me, something I didn't need him to do.

"Build it in."

"I can't do that, Lib."

"Sure, you can, and without a doubt, you should. Inflate the prices of everything. The government does." Libby and her conspiracy theories.

"They absolutely do not."

"Oh, they do." She bobbed her head. "In Independence Day that guy said they charged twenty thousand bucks for a hammer, and thirty grand for a toilet seat."

"That's a movie."

"But there's truth in there, somewhere, right?" Her lower lip extended in a wee pout, and suddenly I knew exactly where Vera had picked it up.

I narrowed my eyes. "I can't charge him more just because."

Her voice was as solid as a fir tree. "Oh yes, you can. And you should. Stick it to him. He's a rich business guy, he can afford it, and he gets a tax break. Why do you think he was so concerned about it being a local business? Government subsidies for the rich."

She had a point, a small one, but a point, nonetheless. I wouldn't be sticking it to him per se, but to his business, and no doubt, there was some kind of tax relief in it for that. "Well... You're definitely onto something."

"I know I am. You can get revenge on him. Seven years in

the making." She leaned back and shook her fists in the air while letting out an evil cackle.

"You need help." However, I couldn't stop the smile from spreading across my face as she drummed her fingers together. "I don't know if I agree with the whole financial revenge idea, but I'll give it some serious consideration."

"Do it!" She cackled again and walked back to her table.

What was the harm if it was a little higher priced? It's not like he'd ever find out, right?

Chapter Three

Sitting at the kitchen table, I placed my aching head into the palm of my hands. It was nearing ten, almost bedtime, but I couldn't sleep just yet. Libby's idea circulated in my head like a Dremel tool at high speed. Part of me disagreed with boosting his price, but the other part – the one that got royally screwed over – that part wanted revenge. Big time. However, crunching the numbers, even if I did bump the fees, it wouldn't make up for all I'd lost, but it would help.

I had lost my job and nearly lost my apartment. But the scariest part was the emotional damage done – I'd been so violently ill, I thought I was going to lose my baby too. As did the doctors. Thankfully, I didn't, and my family pitched in to help, but still. Scary to think how close to rock bottom I'd actually gotten – all over an improperly prepared chicken wrap.

Tipping my head back and staring at the dried water stain on the ceiling, I threw my question into the universe.

"Should I bump his fee because it's him? Should I?"

Not expecting an answer, I sighed and closed my laptop. Perhaps a night of sleep would shed some light on it.

Francesca, my twenty-six-year-old sister, sauntered into the kitchen bright and early for a Monday morning. She poured herself a coffee from the fresh pot I'd just made and sat at the table.

Her perkiness was brighter than the sun, and I suspected my other sister, Mia, was rubbing off on her. They got all the sunshine, and I got all the rain, metaphorically speaking.

"Are you doing the lab trip today, or am I?"

I grabbed the schedule off the side of the fridge, completely forgetting about Vera's blood draw today as part of her annual physical. "Shit."

"It's all good. I don't mind."

The appointment was at one, but at the hospital in Spirit Bay, since they had the best pediatric lab tech in the area.

"Know what, I can take her. I'll be back in time from the consult to pick her up from camp and take her to the lab." I set a reminder on my phone. "I'll just pack her a lunch too."

Yesterday, I'd caved and set up an appointment with David Dean for his customized artwork for ten-thirty this morning.

Taking Libby's advice, and assuming he approved the

project, I'd inflate his prices. Marginally. Not enough that he should turn me down, but if he did end up haggling, at least I wasn't going to take it out of my actual costs.

"Well, if you need help…" Francesca set her black coffee down.

"I know, and I love you for offering."

She'd been a huge help already. After she and her long-time guy split up a year ago, she understandably didn't want to move back home with Mom and Dad and couldn't afford her own place on her meager salary, so instead, moved into the spare room in my house. She helped cook and clean and paid a modest rent payment each month, but more importantly, she became a friend and confidant to me, now that we were older and the age gap wasn't as noticeable. Plus, she and Vera had the best relationship. I loved how Vera adored her auntie, and the two of them always had some secret adventure every Saturday while I was at the market.

"I'm just saying, I'm here if you need me. Don't let your stubborn pride get in the way." Francesca turned her head as my sleepy-eyed daughter dragged herself into the kitchen.

Hair matted on the left side of her head, Vera slumped into a chair beside Francesca and released a slow, drawn-out breath. Turning to me, she whined in a voice that was becoming more and more high pitched as the days went by. "No camp."

I tapped my ear, fingers and hands moving as I spoke. "Where's your aid?"

"Bathroom."

"Go." I signed.

I'd been working on sign language with her since she was first diagnosed with hearing loss as a toddler, and now at almost seven, she was fluent in ASL, a skill she'd need. Her audiologist predicted by age ten, if not sooner, she'd be completely deaf, and no hearing aid in the world would help. According to her doctor, her hearing loss was so profound that right now, when she was just two feet in front of me, it sounded like I was talking through a wall layered in absorbent foam rather than not at all. She was dependent on lip reading, and sign language, especially when her listening device was absent.

For now, the strongest hearing aid I could purchase only helped a little, and the staggering cost of the latest bill was sitting unpaid on my credit card.

Vera returned in a minute with the beige devices nestled into her ear canals.

When she spoke, it was high-pitched, and I often wondered if she could hear the sound of her own voice as clearly as we did. "I don't wanna go to camp."

"You're going. Sorry, Vee, but I know you'll have fun. You've been looking forward to it."

"Aww."

It was a half-day scientist camp at the public library, and the price had been ridiculously cheap that it would've been a sin to not have signed up Vera.

Francesca piped up and signed as she spoke. "Why don't you grab your hairbrush, and I'll do your hair Rey style? And then you'll be the coolest kid at camp."

"Can I bring BB8?" Vera's gaze jumped from Francesca to me.

I nodded, speaking as I signed. As long as she didn't lose her toy, it didn't bother me. "Of course."

"Yay." With a jump from her chair, she nearly launched herself down the hallway and ran back into the bathroom.

"Any bets on if she'll wear her Rey wear?" I sent a questioning eyebrow raise to Francesca.

My sister nodded. "No bets needed, she will."

Vera was obsessed with Rey from the Star Wars movies. I'd managed to find her a costume at a garage sale at the start of summer, and it was one of the only Halloween costumes that was wearing out from wear.

While Francesca did her hair and sang a song in a deep voice, I made Vera's breakfast and packed her lunch. In addition to her hearing loss, she also had dietary restrictions and was allergic to practically everything under the sun. Finding products that lacked soy, peanuts, shellfish, and wheat was hard in the small town, so I often had to make the drive to Courtenay, a few hours away, and stock up. Those trips were costly, as gas on the island wasn't as cheap as on the mainland, and because the food products were more specialized, naturally, they were more expensive. Money just wasn't a luxury I had, but I also didn't need Vera spending more time in the hospital.

Taking the custom order with a nice markup, from the guy who'd nearly cost me everything, just made it feel like Karma was standing in the room laughing her fool head off. I had to be nuts to accept it, right?

At ten-thirty-five, five minutes later than the agreed-upon meeting time, I arrived at Birch Bay Burgers, a restaurant I'd avoided over the last seven years. I'd even avoided coming over to this part of the peninsula just as an extra precaution.

"We're not open yet." A perky young lady dressed all in black had spoken as I approached the hostess stand.

"I have an appointment with Mr. Dean."

"Oh, are you interviewing for the server position?" There was a slight inflection in her voice.

I shook my head. I was most definitely not here for that position; I'd have to be pretty damn desperate to work for the guy. Plus, I wasn't willing to parade around in skintight clothes, with gals who were ten years younger. My style was more like capris and a flowy top, if I left the workshop, not clothing worn as a second skin.

"Who are you then?"

"Erin Normandy – the woodcarver." I attempted to smooth

my frizzing hair.

The humidity in the bay area was rising, and I should've tied it up in, at the very least, a ponytail, but I'd followed Francesca's advice and left it down to look more professional.

"Oh-kay." She spun on her high heels and wiggled her way to a door, disappearing behind it.

While I waited, I checked out the space since it had been a while. It was bright and airy, with the morning sun highlighting the patio area out beyond the bank of windows showcasing the ocean.

As I twisted to see more, Mr. Dean walked out from a short hallway beside the kitchen.

"Ah, hello." His voice bounced off the walls as he extended a hand in greeting, after first checking his watch.

Yeah, I was a few minutes late.

Dressed in a crisp blue shirt with the top button undone and dark dress pants, he oozed professional, and damn, if he wasn't good-looking too. His beard was neatly manicured, and the wrinkles around his eyes were a little deeper as if he'd had a rough night.

"Thank you for coming by. I appreciate you fitting me into your busy schedule."

After squeezing my bones together in a crushing handshake, I broke eye contact and glanced around, hoping no permanent damage happened to my throbbing hand. Despite his rugged good looks, Mr. Dean needed some work in the gentle approach department.

"No problem. It'll help me get an appreciation of the space you're looking at for your artwork, Mr. Dean."

"Please, call me David, Mr. Dean was the principal." Like warm brandy, his voice was soothing. "And my uncle."

I wanted to laugh. "Wait a sec, was he at SS High?"

"Ah, you've met the man."

"Many times over my high school career." Don't know how I didn't make the connection, although he was a gentle principal, warm and caring, not callous and untoward like his nephew before me. I shook away the thought. I was here for a consult, not to compare him to members of his family.

"This is what I had in mind." David stepped around the podium and over to the entranceway, towering over me.

With zero lack of self-control, I checked out his rear view. Those dress pants hugged him in all the right places. Nice. One point for him, even if he was still deep in the negatives because of his total lack of sympathy years back.

David interrupted my tallying as he faced me. "Actually, I had two ideas, but you being the artist, perhaps you can walk me through one or the other or both if the price is right."

I was all ears and reached into my cross-body bag for a notepad. "Tell me what your vision is."

"Okay." He stood in front of a wall, arms extended. The entrance wasn't spectacular - just a plain painted wall with a giant black logo on it. "This all needs to go. It's been here since I opened

33

and blah. I'm tired of looking at it. I want something fresh and new."

I nodded. "And what were you thinking of in its place?"

"Well, that's where you come in. Could you do a mural or something? I was thinking like a carved-out beach on the bottom, some houses or businesses like a skyline of the area kind of thing, include one of the lighthouses, maybe some trees. Make it a focal point. Sometimes the waits are long, and I'd love to have something amazing for people to look at, maybe find hidden items within."

Good grief. I wasn't that great an artist. Not to burst my own bubble, because I knew I had talent, but I wasn't *hidden items within* talented. At least not on purpose. I inhaled and surveyed the wall. It was huge. Much bigger than the four-by-three size I thought he wanted. The cost of materials alone would be staggering.

"Can I measure? To help with the estimate?"

"Please do." The phone attached to his belt rang. "Excuse me a minute."

I pulled out my measuring tape, glad I brought the heavy-duty one as it was longer, and measured the length and the height, making notes in my notepad as I went along. I'd have to break the artwork into segments as I didn't have the space to do something so large, but it was definitely workable, especially incorporating his vision of different scenes. Like the small artwork I did for Dr. Chloe Tarkin, but on a much grander scale. Scratching the measurements down, I added his ideas as well, and drew out a quick design, so I wouldn't forget.

David walked back, leaning over my shoulder as I wrote. "Don't forget the beach idea."

I breathed in a heady, woody scent. It was intoxicating as hell, if not a little overpowering.

"Got it." I added a starfish to help cement it for him.

"Excellent."

Trying not to roll my eyes at his controlling nature, I took a hard blink. "You said you had two ideas?"

"Oh yeah." He stepped away and walked into the dining area, gesturing for me to follow. "This one is a little more out there, but I'm shutting down the dining area for October and overhauling everything."

Had there been another slew of food poisoning complaints? I hadn't heard anything through the gossip queens, and word would spread quickly through the town if there were. Had I gone public with my food poisoning, no doubt he would've done something. But that wasn't who I was, I was the more passive-aggressive type.

David carried on, oblivious to my thoughts. "Private booths will go along that back wall, and I figured I'd like some of those tree pieces you did to go against those walls, one in each booth. But smaller. Say about half the height of what you did for Chloe?" He said her name so casually, I assumed he knew her personally, as most people referred to her as Dr. Tarkin.

"Sure, I can create that no problem." Those were pretty easy in comparison to the mural, which would be a huge undertaking, with likely an even bigger payout. "How many booths were you thinking?"

Tipping his head to the side, he tucked one hand under his arm as the other settled against his chin. His perfectly coiffed head bounced along as I assumed he counted. "There will be seven new seating areas being constructed."

"Seven," I repeated, writing it down. Seven of those pieces alone was great, and I tried to keep my excitement in check. "Time frame?"

"I'd like those before the renos are open, so end of October."

Totally doable for the table pieces. "And the mural? What kind of time frame are you projecting for that?"

"We're having the grand re-opening on Halloween, so before that. Is that a problem to have them all done by then?"

"I will take a look at what customs are on my list, and see where I can fit in the mural, as I suspect the time involved will be much greater, and considering the short time frame, I may have to put a rush on it." I jotted down mid-October for the due date. I hated waiting until the last possible minute for things, and couldn't do that to a customer, so if he wanted Halloween, I was going to have it ready two weeks beforehand, if I could. "Anything else?"

He stepped closer, his cologne wrapping around me and bringing me in fast. His eyes were mahogany, edged beautifully with ebony lashes. But it was the beard that had the strangest effect on me, and deep down I wondered if it would feel scratchy or soft against my delicate skin.

Whoa, wait a minute. I wasn't supposed to be charmed by this guy. He'd cost me too much. Remembering that whole situation – his angry tone, the callous laughter, and his clipped words telling me to get lost, suddenly kiboshed the sex appeal. As the Northern Pikes would say, 'S*he ain't pretty, she just looked that way.*'

Squaring my shoulders, I shook my head and tapped my pencil against the notepad. "If you'd like to go ahead, I can draw up the ideas and get you an estimate on the cost. There's a cost for that design process, and it will be copyrighted."

"Why's that?" There was a slight tip of his head.

"So you don't take my idea to someone else to create." I put on what Libby called my professional, yet sassy-type smile. Not that I had ever run into someone stealing my ideas before, I wasn't about to start, but he was a shrewd enough businessman to find someone else and undercut me.

He chuckled though, and the right side of his cheek pushed up with a grin. "That's fair."

"If you choose to go ahead with the design, I'll deduct the cost of the estimate off the total. There is a 50% deposit required to get started, with the remainder due at the time of delivery. Should you choose to cancel, you'll get back half of the deposit, minus any incurred material expenses."

"You're pretty thorough, Miss?" He trailed off.

I realized I hadn't ever given him my full name. How foolish of me. "Normandy. But you can call me Erin."

"Normandy?" He rocked back on his feet, putting a little distance between us.

Did he remember my name from the food poisoning? I didn't recall ever having given it to him back then.

"As in Adam's little sister, the guy who runs the bookstore?"

I sighed with relief. In our small town, it's no surprise with the familiar last names. "No, that's Francesca."

"Well, there's no way you're older than Adam." It was said with enough charm to soften my rough edges.

"Older and wiser." Much wiser but only twenty-one months older.

"Erin." His expression softened. "I like that name, and it suits you."

Fighting to control my blush, remembering the reason I wasn't supposed to like this guy, I inhaled. Instead, I shrugged as casually as I could. "Thank you. My parents named us well, and we grew into them. My youngest brother is a wild one, so it's fitting he's named Harrison, and Francesca, well, she's the fun one, and Mia? Well, everyone loves her. My name is pretty low-key, and I tend to keep to myself."

His gaze raked over my body. "Yeah, I can see that about you. You seem like the quiet, introspective type."

Not sure if his statement was offensive or not, I backed away, pulling my scratched-out ideas closer to my chest. "So, we're good?

I can go and draw up the designs?"

He uncuffed his sleeve and rolled it up his muscular forearm, giving me what Chloe called arm porn. She was right though, there was something about that look.

With a quick clearing of his throat, he nodded. "I do believe so. I'd be delighted to see what you can create."

I needed to tear my gaze away from the well-defined arm and remember how to breathe. Blinking rapidly, I ran over my scribbled notes to make sure I had everything. "Perfect. And where can I invoice for the estimate?"

Lifting a finger, he sauntered over to the hostess stand, reached inside, and produced a business card. "Here's my card."

"Thanks, I already have it." I opened up my notebook and tapped the card paperclipped to the top.

"Oh, excellent. You can invoice the email listed and call me if you have any questions."

Oh, I had questions, but none that related to this consultation.

"Thank you very much for your business, David." I extended my hand, preparing for his squeeze of pain. Instead, it was a much gentler shake, and I sighed with relief.

"Truly, the pleasure is all mine."

My heart stuttered. Scrambling, I dug through my bag for a business card, unable to locate one. "You have my number, right?"

"Yes, ma'am." He held my gaze for a heartbeat.

What was wrong with me? This man nearly destroyed my

life. Why was my body being such a traitor, warming all over from his intense look?

I swallowed and started toward the main entrance. "Perfect. I'll invoice you tonight and draw up the ideas today and tomorrow, along with a rough estimate in cost."

"Rough?"

"Typically, I'm within 5% of my estimate, and if I'm over, I'll eat the difference." But I won't be with him. My inflated costs, as per Libby's idea, would give me a lot of breathing room.

"Sounds fair."

I put my things away. "I'll be in touch."

My hand was on the door, pushing it open when he quickly approached me. "Wait. Can I interest you in lunch?"

"Here?" The word was out before I could stop myself. Of course it was a stupid thing to say.

"Yes." There was a smirk in his eyes, but it was laced with confusion. "My treat."

My gaze fell to his polished shoes. "I'd love to, but I have somewhere I need to be."

He shuffled. "Fair enough. Raincheck, Erin?"

Why was the way he said my name making my breath catch? I swallowed. "Sure."

We'd have to eat elsewhere though, as there was no doubt in my mind I wouldn't be dining in his establishment. Once was enough.

Chapter Four

Crumbling the piece of paper, I tossed it into the recycle bin set up beside the garbage receptacle. "I swear I'm never going to get this right."

A chime rang out as Vera wandered into the garage, Francesca hot on her heels. Since we lived near the wooded entrance on the edge of town, Francesca's former boyfriend had helped to install a sensor that chimed whenever the door of the house opened, and it rang to my phone. If she wandered away and didn't have her hearing aid in, we'd be hopeless in calling out to her and having her hear us, so this gave us a small warning. As her mother, I had to constantly drill this into her as the clock was ticking on her hearing loss. She needed to tell someone when she was leaving. For any reason. And getting her own cell phone so I could track her was out of my budget.

"Hey, honey, what's up?" I signed and spoke.

Vera moved her hands. She pointed to the few tools and chunks of wood I'd let her have. "Can I play?"

"Yes." I made a fist and bobbed it back and forth, then turned to my sister. "What time do you work tonight?"

Vera donned the required apron and eye protection, climbing onto a stool at a table I'd built for her. She never really made anything, at least nothing familiar to me, but she enjoyed using the tools and hammering things.

Keeping her under a watchful eye, I waited for Francesca's answer.

"Seven."

Francesca worked at the Cowboy Den and absolutely hated it, only showing up mere moments before her scheduled shifts. Nightly, she had to push away the groping hands from drunken men, plus she had a dick of a boss who truly didn't care to protect the wait staff. The only thing keeping her from quitting were the tips, which were ridiculously high. It was amazing the shit she put up with for the money.

"I keep telling you, you need to consider what I proposed. It's a win-win for everyone."

"I've been thinking about that." She pulled a stool beside Vera and watched her chip a piece of wood. "She's pretty good."

I brushed my hand over Vera's head and planted a kiss on her forehead. Pressing my ring and swear finger into my palm while splaying out the other three digits, I signed *I love you* to Vera.

Without signing it back, or saying it even, she went back to work.

"Anyway, I've been thinking about your suggestion. Like really thinking." My sister was hunched over the table, and I saw the little girl in her as she looked up at me with her deep blue eyes, a family gene I had not inherited. "And I think I'm going to do it."

"Really?" I wanted to jump up and down with excitement, but I hesitated.

"I've got enough money set aside to put it together in the basement, but that means for the next couple of weeks, I'm going to be painting and decorating." A glimmer of hope brushed across her face.

I beamed. "You're going to be a great dayhome provider."

"You're sure about all this?"

"I see you with her." I gazed lovingly at Vera. "You were a fantastic nanny for the Hartmans."

"And you don't mind me converting the basement into a play space?"

"I wouldn't have offered it up if I did."

Vera and I didn't have that much, having bought the house a couple of years back with my sister Mia's help. She was a realtor, and found the foreclosure, knowing it needed a lot of work – but nothing I couldn't, or my handy family as it turned out, couldn't address. The house had been a labour of love, and when Francesca moved in a year ago, we partitioned her a spare room in the basement and gave her a three-piece bathroom. It was just as much as her house as it was mine.

"Thank you. I'm going to give my two-week notice today. Tell Nathaniel he can stick it where the sun doesn't shine."

"Well, maybe wait until your last shift to do that." I laughed.

She pulled her thick dark hair over her shoulder and braided it with ease, something I'd never been able to do. For whatever reason, doing a braid caused a weird kink to form in my hand. Francesca had become the hair stylist once Vera's hair was long enough to do something with.

"So, while I'm fixing the basement, I won't be as available to watch her." She ran her hand over her niece's back.

"That's okay. We'll manage. But Saturdays?"

"Are you kidding? That's our special day. I'm not giving that up." She glowed. "And she'll have a spot in my space after school too. It'll be great. She can teach them ASL and have a couple of new friends too."

School started in two weeks, and although I wasn't looking forward to it, in a weird way, I was. It meant being back on a regular schedule, and with the bus picking up and dropping off, it gave me a little more free time to work during the day so I didn't have to after she'd gone to bed.

Francesca straightened and tossed her shoulders back. "What are you working on?"

I showed her my rough idea for the mural which had the

length and height dimensions across the side and top, so I knew what space I had to work with.

"Holy shit, that's huge."

"It's going to be the feature piece for the waiting area."

"Wow. And this?" She pulled the drawings for the table pieces. "This looks like that landscape you made for Dr. Tarkin."

"Exactly. Except smaller. To hang above the table."

"Cool beans." She rocked back on her feet in hesitation.

That expression was signature to Francesca, and usually meant there was something else she wanted to say but wasn't sure how. "What did you want to ask me?"

She hung her head. "I feel bad for asking, as I know you're working, but can I leave her with you?"

"You want to leave my own daughter with me? The horror." I threw a hand over my chest and mocked exasperation. "Go. I'm sure we'll be fine."

"Thanks. Going over to the hardware store to select paint colours to match with the area rugs some guy is selling me for cheap."

"Be safe." I waved as she danced out of the workshop.

Pulling up a chair, I watched Vera chip away at her chunk of wood.

"Hey," I signed and said, "That looks like rocks."

She put her hands flat, palm side down and waved them together, like ocean waves. "Beach rocks."

"You're right. Like the ones we saw on glass beach."

It was so simple and yet beautiful. I watched her chip and carve, the rocks coming alive. It was so easy, I just hadn't seen it before, and I could totally add it to the mural, to give it a little 3D effect and depth.

I planted another kiss on Vera's head and went back to designing my sketch.

After watching Moana for the 100th time, I sadly wondered if ten years down the road she'd remember the beats and melodies of the songs she sung offkey to, or whether they would fade away because she could no longer hear them. The thought worried me, and I couldn't imagine what that was like for her. I hoped my voice never faded for her, and I laid beside her, stroking her head and talking to her about when I was her age, until she fell fast asleep.

With her hearing aid on her bedside table, I still tiptoed out of the room, in case the vibrations on the floor caused her to wake. Grabbing my sketch pad and iPad, popping on Netflix as I sat in the weathered, secondhand shop find, to total the cost for the table pieces. At least those were easy. I had all the needed supplies, so my costs were relatively low. It was just time. But there was no way I was letting David know that. Libby's suggestion rang through my head, and I bumped the numbers. The price still looked reasonable, maybe a little on the higher end, but to make it look better, I added in a volume discount, which knocked off a bit – although I was still going to be paid quite handsomely. Maybe I'd be able to address the leak in the ceiling before winter hit.

Satisfied with that, I played around with various ideas, trying out sketch after sketch. I wasn't sure if I was going to be able to do what I wanted, or see his vision through, but I drew out three concepts.

Not set yet on which design I liked more, I decided to toss the idea by him. Along with the cost design process invoice, I constructed an email asking for another quick visit, if he wasn't too busy, as I wanted to go over the ideas in person. I hit send and took a drink of my tea.

My phone buzzed instantly, and his restaurant popped onto the display.

"Hey, Erin, it's David. Hope I'm not catching you at a bad time."

I glanced at the clock hanging in the living room. Wasn't there an unwritten rule about calling after nine? "No, that's fine."

"I figured since I just got your email, you were up."

"It's all good." I put the phone onto speaker and tucked my legs underneath my butt. "Is there anything wrong with the invoice?"

"Oh no, not at all. Just give me a sec." The keys clicked on the other side of the line.

My phone buzzed – invoice paid. "Wow. That was quick."

"No point in delaying that part, so no, the invoice looked

great. You mentioned how you had three ideas for the murals and wanted to get together?"

Opening up a spreadsheet, I marked his invoice as paid.

"I thought I would email you the ideas, if you'd like, and you can look them over and give me the okay or tell me to start over. Once I get approval on what you'd like, then I can draw up the contract with the costs."

The phone became muffled as he spoke, likely talking to a staff member. "Sorry about that. Are you okay if we meet in person to discuss? It's a little hard to go back and forth over email."

"I agree." Which was what I wanted anyhow but didn't want to seem overeager. "Sure. I can pop over tomorrow, around 10:30?"

"That won't work. Are you free tomorrow evening?"

"Let me check." I hopped off the couch and over to the schedule on the side of the fridge where Francesca penciled in her work shifts. I checked tomorrow's date, and she was off; she'd be able to keep an eye on Vera after I tucked her into bed. "I am free. Should I come by after the supper rush, like around 8:30?"

"How about I pick you up and take you someplace nice?"

I swallowed and choked out the words, "Like a date?"

A good-natured laugh rang through the speaker. "Sure, if you'd like." There was such confidence in his voice, as if he was a women magnet and just the mere prospect of meeting with him would spark the interest of the woman.

"Well, I, um." Rational words blew through my brain like a

hurricane. I wanted to say no, but I didn't want to turn down what could also be a huge infusion of funds.

"If the idea of me picking you up doesn't work, and I'll be honest, I'm not offended, let's meet at the Harbour Chophouse?" He offered before I could make my lips form a proper word.

The Harbour Chophouse was a steak place, an *expensive* steak place. However, it could be a business expense, and a write-off at the end of the year, if I could manage to float the money for it until then.

Somehow, my head took control and nodded.

"Erin, are you still there?"

Thinking fast, I blurted out, "Yes. Sorry, bad connection."

"Whew. So tomorrow, Chophouse, seven-thirty?"

I'd be a fool to say no, so I did the only acceptable thing I could do. I agreed.

Chapter Five

*F*rancesca's voice pierced the air. "He invited you to the Chophouse?"

"Yeah. It's no biggie." But I was brushing the whole idea off or trying to.

To me, it was a business meeting. He was going to drop big money on a project, and he wanted to make sure we were both getting all the details right.

"His place is a family restaurant, nothing wrong with meeting there. When you go on a date, you go to the Chophouse." Francesca spun around my room, landing on my bed. "And you. Are not. Wearing that."

"What's wrong with this?" Capris and a top, standard Erin wear, and standard business date attire. "I could wear my overalls and tank top."

"I wouldn't let you leave the house *on a freaking date*

wearing those ratty clothes." Francesca leaned back on my bed and tossed her hands into the air.

"It's not a date, that's where you're wrong."

She rolled into a sitting position. "Oh, but it is."

Firm in my stance, I placed one foot forward and crossed my arms over my chest. "I'm not trying to score a date with this guy. It's totally business related. Adam does this kind of thing all the time."

"Yeah? And look where that got him. He's now dating his event coordinator."

I wrinkled my nose. "Fair point, but…" Where was I going to go with this? "My point is I'm not looking for a long-term relationship, hell, I'm not even looking for a date. I'm not interested, especially in him."

She fell back on my bed. "It's been years since you've had a man in the house. It's time to move on."

"Man in the house? This isn't even a date!"

"It's time to get laid, Erin. You need it. It's been far too long."

I choked on my own spit. "It hasn't been that long."

Seven years wasn't a long time, right? Afterall, I went twenty-two years once, I could wait until Vera was much older.

"All guys aren't like him, you know." She didn't need to name him, we all knew who the *him* was. He who shall never be named.

"Says who, you? Wasn't Tristan exactly like him?"

Well, maybe not exactly, and I prayed to God Francesca

never had to deal with the likes of Vera's father and family. In addition to hurting the guy that harmed Francesca, Adam would lose his freaking mind, and he'd already spent enough time in jail for protecting his girlfriend. Although Summer was a smart cookie and escaped before harm fell on her, she also believed I didn't know the truth, but Cheshire Bay was a small town, and gossip travelled fast.

"Fine, Tristan was a jerk, you happy?"

"No, not really." I sat beside her on the bed and swiped the bangs away from her eyes. "I want you to be happy, and you deserve a guy who treats you with respect."

"Wow, aren't you a little pot calling the kettle black?"

"My time is done. My dating years are far behind me. I have a child who deserves all of me."

"Oh my god. You act like you're ninety. You're thirty-three."

I brushed off her comment. "Vera needs me."

"I think Vera would want you to be happy." Francesca walked to the door. "If you're not going to change, at least do something with your hair. Maybe you're not interested in him, but you can dazzle him with your beauty, and make him fall under your spell. Then he'll pay any price you ask." Her hand gripped the door frame. "Have fun tonight. Enjoy yourself."

With that, she wandered down the hall, and I stared at my reflection. Maybe she was right? Maybe I could go out and have a good time and put a wee bit of effort into my looks.

I'd changed into a dress and put my curly hair into a low,

twisty bun, allowing a few shorter tendrils to escape and frame my face. I even swiped a smidge of foundation onto my skin and ran some dark green eyeliner around the edges of my eyes; it made the hazel colour pop. After dotting my lips with a smear of lipstick, I snuck into Vera's room and stole a dab of her dollar store perfume. At least it was something, and it smelled like caramel.

Francesca's eyes widened as big as her growing smile when I joined her and Vera in the living room. "That's what I'm talking about."

"You look gorgeous." Francesca tapped Vera and signed. "Doesn't your mommy look pretty?"

She put her hand into a number five position, with her thumb touching her chin, and waved her fingers across her face until they touched her thumb. "Pretty."

"Thank you." I curtsied and planted a kiss on Vera's forehead. "I won't be out late."

"Take your time, I won't wait up." She wiggled her brows.

I playfully smacked her across the shoulders. Signing *I love you* to them both, I drove across town to Harbour Chophouse.

After walking into the fancy, high-end restaurant and inhaling the scent of spicy, grilled meat, I glanced around looking for David. He was nowhere to be seen. A wild feeling that I'd been stood up started to brew in my gut.

"Can I help you?" The hostess asked.

"I'm just waiting for someone."

"Can I seat you until they arrive?"

That would've been rude, so I shook my head. "No, thanks. I'll just wait."

Of course, I was a few minutes late, but that hadn't meant David needed to leave, right?

A co-worker beside her tapped on the iPad. "Are you waiting for a guy?"

I'd hoped I kept my eye rolling internal. "Maybe."

Her voice pitched in curiosity, as she slowly hesitated in asking, "Are you Erin, by chance?"

"Yes." My eyes narrowed.

"Perfect. He's already waiting for you."

Really? Wow. Guess that ruled out a date-date, didn't it? Shouldn't the guy be standing at the front, and escort the lady through the place? Perhaps it had been a long time since I'd been out there.

"This way please."

The Harbour Chophouse was a small, cozy restaurant with a killer view as it sat perched on a little outlet with a 310° view of the ocean. Three-quarters of the dining area was flanked by huge windows, and beyond a set of French doors leading to an outdoor seating area, there was a scattering of tables, a few to give the illusion of total privacy.

That's where the hostess led me.

She stopped in front of a table for two, one that was pushed against the bank of windows, where only a slight ocean breeze circulated, and above was a pergola, with a roll-out shade, although tonight it was open to the clear skies above.

"Ah, my apologies." David, dressed in a fine dress shirt with his cuffs rolled back, set down his phone, rose, and stretched out his hand.

I shook it and took the only other seat across from him. Tucking my dress under me, I sat, and David did the same.

The hostess handed me my leather-bound menu. "May I grab you a drink from the bar?"

"I'm fine with a chamomile tea."

David tapped his glass. "I'm having a beer."

It looked so good too; a dark amber, slight head. "Sure, I'll have what he's having."

A faint smile warmed his façade. "My apologies for not meeting you at the front. I had a quick staff issue to deal with, and the hostess promised she'd bring you back."

"It's all good."

"Please don't think me a rude host, being that I invited you and all."

"Honestly, it's all good. It's not like it was a date-date. It's a business date." I shut my mouth before it could run away and say something even stupider. "Anyway, it was no big deal. I likely would've done the same."

"Good." He took a sip of his drink, and a splash of foam hung on the tip of his whiskers. "Good." He pushed the menu off to the side. "I'm a creature of habit, and I always order the same thing. I don't know why Ruby always insists on bringing me a menu."

"You come here often?"

He leaned closer and whispered. "Is it weird that I do?"

I shook my head, even if it was a little unusual.

"At my place, the staff are always brown-nosing and trying to be perfect, even though I've seen them on the floor. I hate them waiting on me, and I'd rather not meander through the kitchen getting in anyone's way." He rested back against his chair. "I even bring my own lunch on occasion to eat at my desk."

Not that I blamed him. I certainly hadn't eaten there in seven years. The cook needed to brush up on what was an acceptable level for cooking meat and should definitely invest in a meat thermometer because eye-balling it didn't work.

"What are you going to have?" David took another drink of his beer.

"Oh, I don't know. It's so rare for me to go out."

"May I make a suggestion?"

I searched his face, waiting to see a sign of dominance or misogyny or anything that would send up a red flag. There was nothing.

"Do you like seafood? The Pistachio Crusted Salmon is to die for." He nodded.

"Your go-to choice?"

"Sometimes, but not lately. I'm having the New York Striploin."

Perusing the menu, I found it. One rule I learned was to never order a restaurant item that cost more than the person who invited you, so I needed to keep things under that price. However, it seemed that his selection was one of the most expensive entrees, so my options were plentiful.

"Tough choice?" He playfully cocked an eyebrow and twisted in his seat.

"Very much."

Our server, who introduced himself as Tim, set down my beer. "Are you ready to order? Or shall we start with an appetizer?"

Before I had a chance to speak, David spoke. "How about the Neptune Mushrooms and the Scallops & Bacon?"

I scoured the menu quickly and tried to keep my thoughts in line. Holy shit they were pricey appetizers, and combined with the drinks… Yikes. It was going to be a super pricy night out, even just covering my half of the bill.

"Excellent choice, sir." He turned to me. "Are you ready to order?"

"Too many decisions." And mental math was starting to wear me down.

"If you aren't a steak and seafood person, the blackened chicken is good, right Tim?"

He nodded. "The best."

"I don't eat chicken." It was so easy to let it spill out, I forgot for a moment who I was dining with. Seeing the questioning expression tugging on his eyes, I closed the menu. "You know what, the Teriyaki Sirloin will be perfect, thank you."

It was also the cheapest thing on the menu, so I could cover my portion of the bill. But damn, it was going to be tight. May need to push back a few upcoming purchases until they became a definite need.

Tim took David's order and walked back into the dining room.

Soft orchestra music played overhead, fitting with the general ambience of the place.

"You said you'd been sketching out some ideas, may I see them?"

"Oh, of course." I pulled out my portfolio and set it over my placemat. I withdrew the first one and handed it over. "It's not perfect but should give you a rough idea of what I'm going to build." It was a combination of designs, and it didn't float my boat so to speak, but it had potential.

David barely gave it a passing glance.

"Then I thought of this. It's a little smaller, but more focalized on a landscape." I tapped a different part of the picture as I explained what would be carved out, making use of the negative space and what would be added to give it depth.

"It's good. I like this one more than the first."

I swallowed, worried about the next drawing. "And then I was inspired to create this. And it's much easier to do because it takes the elements of the table pieces, with all their layerings, and scales it up." I set the rough sketch in front of him, watching as he inhaled sharply and studied it.

"May I?" He touched the paper.

"Of course."

Lifting it up, he stretched out his arm and stared, tilting the sketch. "I like this one."

Once he set it back down, I explained how I'd construct it, and how it would need to be assembled. I was practically tripping over my words. The grand idea was so similar in concept to the table pieces that the mural really helped bridge the connection.

With a faint smile, he agreed it was perfect. "I like your enthusiasm since I know that with it, you'll be quite involved in the concept, all the way through to the finished project."

"Yes. Once the idea hit me, I couldn't stop. It was easy in my mind to see how it would all come together."

"And project timing? When could this be completed?"

I squared my shoulders. I'd be able to budget my time well, and still create new pieces for the farmer's market, but it would occupy a fair chunk of time. "My goal is mid-October, seven weeks from now, and I'd install it as well."

"That won't be necessary."

59

"I don't mind. I'd hate for someone else to try and assemble it only for them to crack it or something bad to go wrong." And I'd be out the money to repair it. "I promise a finished project and to give it to you in pieces for someone else to put together, well, it doesn't feel right."

"Fair enough." He took a sip of his beer and handed me back the drawing, his fingers grazing against mine like a shot of static electricity.

It caused me to stare at our brief connection. My heart hammered in my chest. It wasn't supposed to do this, get all excited by a simple little touch, and yet I swore it was beating hard enough to make my shirt dance.

David raked his gaze up to my eyes. "And dare I ask what this particular piece will set me back?"

From under the drawings, I pulled out the itemized list for the project he selected. Naturally, it had been the most expensive one, so first I softened him up with the table pieces and a slight flutter of my eyelashes, the way Francesca had instructed me to flirt a little to make it easier. I felt utterly foolish.

"Let me show you the table pieces first."

Our server arrived and set down two steaming plates of appetizers. The scents were mouthwatering, and I couldn't wait to sink my teeth into one of the bacon-wrapped scallops.

I set out the table pieces, each a different element of the grand mural.

"Ooh, I like that idea." He plated some appetizers for me. "Dig in. They're better warm."

I popped one into my mouth and sighed with each heavenly bite. I wiped my mouth before speaking. "And here is the cost."

"Each? Or total?" His eyes bugged out for a fraction of a second.

"Oh, gosh, sorry that's the total for the seven pieces." I pointed to a line further down. "That's the breakdown per item."

A gentle whew blew out of him. Suddenly, I was worried he was going to reject the mural.

"And this is the cost for the mural." I slid him the paper with the estimated labour hours, and the cost of materials while I munched on a mushroom stuffed with crab and cream cheese.

He grabbed a scallop while reading over the invoice.

Time seemed to slow down, and I finished another mushroom before he finally spoke.

"This is a little steep."

Which I knew because I'd inflated the price like Libby said, but it wasn't astronomical the way she wanted. I only added in what I'd lost in wages because of his poor food handling practices, and that price hadn't even been adjusted for inflation, however, I did add a tiny five percent increase to my hourly wage and a ten percent upcharge on the materials.

He didn't need to know I got a deal at the hardware store, not the one in Cheshire Bay because they were too expensive, but rather at the national chain in Courtenay, a few hours drive away.

"May I think on this? It was a little higher than what I'd been preparing for."

"Oh, of course."

"Can I keep this?"

"Absolutely."

Beads of sweat built across the nape of my neck. Was he going to compare prices and ask me to price match? I hoped not. It was crazy to think but once the design popped into my head, it was all I could think about, and adding up the cost versus what I was charging him was going to provide a nice little cushion for Vera and me, something we'd never really had.

"Let me think on it for the next couple of days, and I'll get back to you by Friday." His phone vibrated on the table, grabbing his attention.

"That's fine." My mouth started to dry out, and I took a ladylike sip of the beer, which helped. I grabbed another mushroom and popped it into my mouth. I'd been foolish in thinking I was going to get away with it. No doubt, he'd call me up on Friday and tell me he's going to go a different direction.

David cleared his throat and grabbed his phone. "Forgive me, I just need a minute." His thumbs typed frantically, and when he finished, set it screen side down. "Well, that concludes the business portion of the evening." Tucking the estimate into the inside pocket of his suit jacket hanging over the back of his chair, he returned his attention to me. Fully and undivided, with his hand on the beer and his gaze set on me. "Let's get to the real reason I invited you out."

I swallowed and crossed my legs together at the ankles, my heart hammering loudly as I leaned in just ever so closer.

"There's something I need to find out."

Chapter Six

I took in the man sitting across from me; handsome and charming, in a way I didn't see coming, and yet, here was the guy who nearly ruined my life. Or at least was a close second.

"What is it you want to know?" I focused on the tip of his nose, then on the small smirk tugging on the left side of his mouth. Inhaling silently, I held my breath.

David relaxed, his broad shoulders sloping downwards. "Tell me about how you came into woodworking."

My breath blew out in one fell swoop. "Okay, that I can answer."

His brows knit together. "Were you worried?"

"I don't talk about my private life to customers." I dug my fingers into my napkin, and chanced a look at his expression, expecting to see something other than genuine concern.

"I can understand that."

"Good." Uncurling my fingers, I reached for a small piece of mushroom and popped it into my mouth. "As far as woodworking goes, to be honest, I sort of fell into it."

"How's that?" He leaned a little closer, wiping his hands on the cloth napkin and leaning onto his forearms.

"Well, a few years back I lost my job." My focus leapt off him and shot over to another table, where I stared with great interest at the couple. "Trying to get back on my feet was difficult, but I managed." The flickering candle on the table danced in the light breeze. "I got a job at the hardware store and was a quick study on using their machines for the customers and figured I could do that on my own." And once I'd given birth to Vera, not leaving my newborn was a huge deal, but I wasn't about to tell him any of that.

Pulling myself up, rather than hunching over, I carried on. "I started small, mostly making picture frames and wooden door signs, but then everyone started doing that as it became a hot new trend. While business was good, I needed to step outside the box and give the consumers something different, so I started making carvings."

"And things grew from that?"

I looked into his face. He was leaning forward and taking in everything I said. "They really did. I was able to quit my part-time job and focus on this full-time."

"That's amazing. You must do well, I assume?"

I shrugged. "I can't afford lavish trips and all that, but I can pay the mortgage and put food on the table, so I consider that a success. The market really helped launch things for me, and I'm forever grateful to Summer for putting it together."

Summer Bates, my brother's girlfriend, had been instrumental in creating a seasonal outdoor marketplace, and it was a huge touristy draw over July and August.

"What will you do in the winter?" He rested his chin in his hand, as a questioning expression settled over him. It was a little unnerving to be the center of attention.

"I will continue to make pieces and get a stock going. I don't have much left, so the pieces I display at the market are fairly fresh, if you will."

"You put your heart and soul into your work. There's no doubt your customers see that too."

A small smile tickled my lips. "I hope so. What about you? You've always worked here?"

He laughed. "No, not always, but I've been invested in the industry since, well, since I graduated high school." He took a sip of his beer and licked his lips. "I worked odd jobs around town, as a teenager typically does, and eventually about twenty years ago I got a job here. Hated the way the place was run, hated my boss, the whole works." He rolled his eyes for good measure. "I saved up, took out a sizeable loan, and ten years ago bought him out. My wife joined me—"

My gaze fell to his hand. There was no ring, and for some stupid reason, my heart hammered with the thought of him being single. Un-attached. Possibly.

"She helped decorate this, but it wasn't the look I wanted, but since her parents were investors, I went with it. I only wanted to run it properly, and as long as the customers were happy, I was too."

"Your wife did a nice job." People loved it, and often raved about the décor, so Mrs. Dean knew what she was doing.

"I can't fault her that."

He missed my subtle subtext and leaned back in his chair, glancing around. "You know, now that I'm taking a good look around, I think she took a few ideas from here and scaled things down to fit our establishment."

"Or maybe this owner saw your place and changed things up a bit? Competition is known for building on another's success."

He grabbed the last mushroom but pushed the last scallop my way. "Maybe. But I like the idea of thinking outside the box. Doing what no one has done."

He pulled his hands off the table when our server appeared with our main courses.

Savoury spices filled the space and the steak looked mouthwatering. I couldn't wait to dive in.

"What can I do that no one has done before? How can I make my restaurant the must-eat at place?"

"Have my artwork hanging?" I laughed at my own question.

"Touché. What about exclusivity?"

"As in your place being the only place I can display my

artwork?" He wasn't serious, was he? Chloe had her piece hanging at her clinic, and there was no way I was going to tell her to take it down.

"Why not?"

"That's so limiting. Imagine if I said you couldn't sell burgers because the diner sold them? And you couldn't sell wine because the Chophouse does?" My feathers were starting to ruffle.

A broad grin spread like wildfire from cheek to cheek. "I was kidding and would never do that to you."

"Oh, okay." I inhaled slowly and eyed him cautiously.

"But I must say I love your passion."

I cut off a sliver of my steak and had a taste. It was so good, and almost took away from the sudden awkwardness of the situation. "Sorry, I just tend to get—"

"Never apologise for being passionate about your work. It's missing in a lot of people these days."

"Really? I don't think so."

"Sure, it is. Most people hate their jobs."

"Do you?" Maybe he threw it out as a line, but I was grabbing onto it.

He set his fork down and the Adam's apple in his throat bobbed. "I didn't use to, but then for a long time, I really did. I hated everything about my job. Eventually though, that feeling went away."

"What changed?"

"I divorced my wife."

"Oh, I'm sorry." And deep down I was. However, my heartbeat also kicked up a notch at the thought of him being single. Even if he wasn't the nicest of people.

"There was a time… a time where I felt I was on top of the world." He paused and looked around. We were alone on the patio, so no one would hear whatever it was he wanted to tell me. "Nothing could bother me, and I was on top of my game. Voted #1 best restaurant in the area, beating out this place. Truly, I was on the best winning streak of my life. Then it all came crashing down, and I had to rebuild my life from the inside out. But from the ashes rose the phoenix."

Something I could totally relate to, and I lifted my beer to clank against his. "To rising from the ashes."

Maybe things weren't what they seemed. Maybe his crashing down coincided with my own and we were more alike than I realized. And maybe, my heart needed a swift kick because there was no way I was supposed to be remotely interested in this guy.

Chapter Seven

*D*eep into another custom piece, this one of a bear, I hardly heard my phone ringing. Until I happened to move my head to admire a sweet carving, and I saw the screen flashing.

I hit the speaker button. "Hello."

"Erin, it's David."

"Oh, hi." I straightened to my full height of five foot three and set down my tools. Oh shit, today was Friday. At least he'd kept his word. I leaned against the table and held my breath.

"I've reviewed your estimate, and I'd like to go ahead."

Yes. I fist-bumped the air. Finally, lady luck was on my side. Taking a sharp but silent breath to control my emotions, I breathed out. "Thank you. I appreciate your business and look forward to constructing your mural."

"I have the deposit all ready for you. Can I swing by your workshop and drop off the contract shortly?"

My workshop was in the garage behind my house, and I wasn't comfortable having customers pop by. "Umm, can I meet you somewhere in an hour?"

There was a brief pause on the line. "I'm actually on my way out of town for the weekend, and just leaving. We can wait until Monday, if that's easier."

If I waited, it took time away from the project, and the deposit now would help soften the blow on Vera's new hearing aid. Tipping my head back, I stared at the ceiling and shook my head. "No, now works. I'm at 24 Wings Gate, my shop is at the back in the garage."

"Perfect. I'm less than five minutes away." Which wasn't surprising. Cheshire Bay wasn't that big a town. However, five minutes didn't give me any time to freshen up and make myself presentable. Damn.

In case he didn't have the contract signed, I needed another ready to go. Flipping through the papers on a makeshift desk covered in a fine layer of sawdust, I dug out a file folder marked contracts and popped the copy into an envelope before the dust in the air had a chance to claim the fresh paper. I had just set it down when through the glass main door, I watched a little green Mini pull into my driveway.

Rather than greet him, and have Francesca walk out at just the perfect time, I let him find his way to the door and knock as the doormat chime sounded his alert. However, he ignored it, knocked, and stepped inside.

His jaw dropped as he closed the door behind him, his left hand tightly gripping a thick envelope.

A quick glance down was all it took to realise I was out of place. Even in my own workspace. My horrid jean coveralls with a rip in the butt and frayed hems matched with a tank top that was originally white, were both a far cry from the business attire two nights ago. That lady and I could've been distant relatives for all the similarities we currently shared.

David looked beyond me, whistling as he checked out my space. "Wow, what a place."

I surveyed the mess, inhaling as I approached. Smelled like someone washed in an expensive cologne, and it should've been offensive, but for some reason, it was intoxicating and warm; like a comforting scent.

"Yeah, it is what it is, but if I were you, I wouldn't come in much further. Wouldn't want to get your pants or shoes dirty."

There was a shine about his footwear that likely came from a solid buffing. Ten feet deeper into my shop, and his work would all be for naught.

He held out the envelope. "The deposit, in cash, and the contract."

"In cash?" That was unusual, given the amount. "Do you mind if I look?" I took the envelope and gently grazed his hand, curious at the little tingles of electricity zapping up my arm.

"And if I said I did?" A coy expression popped his left

eyebrow up. "Don't you trust me?"

"Trust is earned, not freely given out."

He tipped his head to the side, putting his weight on his left foot.

"Do you not check when your customers pay?" At least I said it nicely, with a hint of playfulness.

He nodded. "Fair enough. Go ahead, check, it's all there."

I pulled out a thick stack of twenties, fifties, and a few hundred-dollar bills. There were so many I wanted to protect them like little babies and snuggle them against my chest. It was so much money, and this was just the deposit.

Keeping my calm demeanor in check, I opened the contract and scanned it for anything out of the ordinary. It all looked perfect. And the best part, it was signed.

With a pen in hand, I signed my name at the bottom of one copy and handed it back. "For your personal records."

"Thank you." He stepped closer, and gently touched my hair.

It was weird until he showed me what was between his fingers. A chunk of wood.

Heat singed my cheeks. "That's where that went."

Damn curly hair. Acted like a net every single time.

He handed it to me, and I took it from his hand only to toss it onto the floor where it could party with its friends.

"I'm not a pig, but I do a sweep every night." Meh, it was closer to once a month, but he didn't need to know that.

"I wasn't going to say anything." He threw his hands out in a not-guilty pose.

"And I assure you, it doesn't affect the quality of my work. Constantly cleaning up after myself, well, that's a horse of a different colour." If I had to clean up after every carving or sanding, production would halt, and I didn't have time for that.

"Do you have a website?"

I shook my head, curious where he was going with the question he pulled out of thin air. "Just a Facebook page, or whatever the hell they call it these days, although I have all the social media platforms, I stick to Facebook. I'd rather work and carve and cut than spend hours putting information online. It's like yelling into the void."

Even if Summer would disagree. She had a gift for the whole social media marketing thing, but she also spent all day long on it. There wasn't a lot of personal interaction with her and customers, it was all digital in her world, whereas I preferred getting my hands dirty and one-to-one customer interactions.

"This would make for a neat photo though. Show your fans where the magic happens."

I surveyed the space, trying to see it as a customer would. Would they think it was messy? Would they scour to see neat finds, and several works in progress? I tipped my head from side to side.

"It's not a bad idea."

"And it doesn't have to be anything time-consuming either.

Apparently, the rawer and more real, the more customers like it." He shrugged. "Or so I'm told by my social media rep."

"You have a social media rep?" Why was I so surprised?

He blew out a long breath and shoved his hands into the pockets of his perfectly tailored pants. "Have to, nowadays. A few years back someone, or a group of someones, I'll never know, slammed my social media sites with hate and vulgarity, and claimed I gave them food poisoning."

The heat in my cheeks ratcheted up another hundred degrees.

He was referring to me. Years ago, after I'd recovered physically from my incident, I had created dozens of email and social media accounts and blasted his restaurant with negative reviews. I wasn't kind, but then again, he wasn't either when I'd called to complain, and asked for a mediocre bit of recuperation.

"Wow." It wasn't the best response in my toolbox, but it would have to do.

"Yeah. Health inspectors came out and gave me a solid workout, but they found nothing out of line, and everything was within safe limits. Things settled down for a while, but then it all fired up again so I hired a social media rep to watch my sites so I could take the offense rather than the defense. The hate and lack of response wasn't a good look for the restaurant, but looking back now, maybe not replying to that group worked. Eventually, the hateful comments slowed down. Although one – EatHere&GetSick – still pops up on occasion.

Well, yeah, I couldn't let people forget. And it wasn't that often. My last posting was at least a couple of months ago.

"Did you ever find the person or persons responsible?" I swallowed and held my breath, hoping he hadn't heard the lump go down my throat, and that his answer was no.

"No."

I exhaled.

"And I gave up. Every direction led nowhere."

"That's too bad." Did I sound sincere? I hoped so.

"Anyway, I'm sorry, I got off topic. What were we talking about?" He stared into my eyes, holding me in place.

"Social media. The need for a rep. Weird, unstaged pictures of my workspace." Blinking, I tore my gaze away and over to the carving I had been working on.

"Right." He stepped a little closer and lowered a shoulder, a teasing grin on his lips and a twinkle in his eyes. "Would it be weird if I—"

A doorbell chime sounded out from my phone while also lighting up the display with the notification. Vera had opened the door of the house; she was outside.

I put my hand up to stop David from talking, both grateful for the interruption and a little sad, as I wanted to know the rest of his question. "Sorry, just a second."

The doorbell chimed again as the door to the workshop opened, and my little girl sauntered in, instantly halting in her tracks.

"Who's that?" She vocalized in a high-pitched squeak unrecognizable to most as she signed.

"This is Mr. Dean," I signed his name and carried on. "I'm designing a custom piece for him."

"Nice." Her palms swiped together.

I faced David and stood protectively in front of my child. "This is my daughter, Vera."

I expected a gentle wave and a forced hello, instead, he hunched down to her level, and repeated the gesture back, adding *nice to meet you.*

My jaw hit the floor. He knew ASL.

Francesca burst through the door, sending another set of chimes off. "Ohmygod, I'm so sorry. I was in the bathroom."

Still surprised at the way David interacted with my daughter, I shook my head and stared at my sister, popping on a smile. "It's okay."

"She wanted to know if you wanted to join us for an ice cream with Mia." Francesca signed for Vera's benefit.

I had a pile of projects to finish, but the thought of a sisterly get-together and a lemon crunch ice cream cone was an offer too good to pass up. Even if it was still morning.

"Sure, I'm almost done here." To my daughter, I smiled and signed *ten minutes?*

Vera nodded, and with a skip headed back outside, the doorbell chiming as she left.

My sister lingered and extended her hand. "I'm Fran. Have we met before?"

He pumped her hand. "David Dean, and no, I don't believe so."

I watched in rapt attention, waiting for him to hit on the prettiest Normandy sister, but he didn't. Instead, prim and proper, he returned his hand to his pocket.

"David Dean of Birch Bay Burgers?" Her smile widened and there was a slight spring in her step.

"Does my reputation precede me?" His gaze volleyed between her and me.

"Maybe. You're the one she's planning this huge mural for."

Thank you for not spilling the beans.

"That's me." He had the good sense to let a sly grin tickle the edges of his smile.

"You've picked well. Erin will make something gorgeous for your place. You won't be disappointed."

I might, however, die of embarrassment before the project got finished if she kept going on.

"I honestly don't think that's even a remote possibility. From what I've seen, Erin does impeccable work."

Fran almost seemed to be dancing on the spot.

"Vera?" I questioned, hoping she'd take the hint and follow my daughter back into the house, which still hadn't chimed.

Francesca glanced out the window. "I can see her. She's

checking out the car, but point taken. See you in a few minutes."

I resumed looking at David. Nope, still didn't seem to be falling under my sister's spell. A first for sure.

"Give me ten, and I'll come join you."

She left us, leaving the door wide open.

David stood before me, and in my head, I was practically shouting at him to finish asking what he was going to. Which was crazy, because I wasn't really interested in him, and I had no right to be interested.

"I'll let you finish up, so you can have some ice cream. Oh, get the Lemon Crunch. It's to die for."

"Okay." I breathed the word out. Lemon Crunch was my all-time favourite.

"Would it be weird if I come by on occasion and see how things are going?"

I swallowed, disappointed in how the end of the question went. "Sure. But if you don't mind giving me a heads-up first. Mostly to prepare Vera as she won't likely hear the car pull up."

"Not a problem." He meandered to the door, pausing as he turned around. The morning sun put him into a full eclipse, and it was breathtaking. "Thank you."

"You're welcome. Thank *you* for the business."

"We're going to enjoy this project."

I hope so.

Chapter Eight

ibby bounced around the booth beside me, chatting up every single customer and listening to their life story as she packaged their pastries and cookies. The perk of having a consumable product – customers always wanted more. Each time, she'd waved them off with a *come back soon* and the friendliest smile that should be part of a welcoming package to the area.

Not the case with my display, however, I wasn't hurting for sales today. My big pieces of the week – framed miniature versions of the layered artwork I'd made for Chloe – all sold out before noon. I'd taken the liberty of trying my hand at social media again, and posted a few dozen pictures to my page, adding they'd only be available at the market. All I had left, aside from whale tail carvings in various sizes and a couple of unpainted lighthouses, were a few signs from back in the day that I'd found in storage when I was cleaning the shop. They sat untouched, as they'd been overdone a couple years back. Whimsical Whims, on Main Street, sold them regularly, so they really weren't anything unique for me to offer to customers.

"Ooh, I like this." An older woman stopped at my booth and picked up a lighthouse.

Having watched Libby chat off everyone's ear, I was going to try her trick and add a fun story to it. Nothing ventured, nothing gained, right?

"That is based off the lighthouse situated at the southern tip of Cheshire Bay. Have you ever been?" I asked, watching her face for interest.

"No, not yet."

I glanced at her hand. There was a ring on her finger.

"It's the most romantic place in all the bay area. My fiancé proposed to me on bended knee in front of one, right as the moon was rising." My right hand covered my chest as I sighed. "It was impossible to say no."

"Wow." She searched my hand, looking for the absent engagement ring. "Did you get married there too?"

"We haven't set a date."

"And it's a functioning lighthouse?"

There were a few decommissioned scattered along the coastline on our little peninsula, but this one was a fully working one, complete with a grounds crew. I nodded.

"I'll take it, and maybe convince my husband to come and

check it out in the real." She dug into her purse and presented me with the cash.

"Make sure you pack a picnic supper and go when the clouds are scattered. It makes for the most beautiful insta-worthy pictures."

"I will, thanks. Good luck with your wedding."

It worked. Although in hindsight, she may have been a little too old for Instagram, but you never knew. Handing back her change and watching her walk away, I pulled out another lighthouse and set it in its place. They were older items, not up to the caliber of work I did now, so they sold at a discount, but whatever, it was extra cash in my pocket.

"Okay, you've been holding out on me. Fiancé? Lighthouse?" Libby wandered over to my side, tugging on her blue-tipped braids. "Do dish. I want all the details. How did I not know you were engaged?"

"Because I'm not now." I hadn't thought she'd heard, and if I knew that were a possibility, I would've used a different story. There were so many to choose from.

She scrunched up her face. "I'm sorry. Was it Vera's father?"

I moved a whale tale to the front of my table, and repositioned a lighthouse beside it, making sure my book of custom designed pieces was front and centre.

"I'm sorry. You don't have to talk about it." Her tone softened, along with her shoulders.

"Good, because I can't."

It was long and complicated, and no longer worth my time. I hated the man immensely but loved the best gift he'd ever given me – Vera. The asshole, and his righteous little family, were no longer welcome in any of our lives, and the court ordered restraining order backed that up. Once he signed over his parental rights, we went an extra step and had his name removed from Vera's birth certificate, mainly to protect Vera. Having him pay child support and Vera's medical bills would be welcome, but not at the cost of my mental health. It's enough that his family put a huge down payment on our house, but I've always considered that hush money.

The doorbell chime sounded through my wireless headphones, and I threw my gaze to the clock on the wall. Francesca and Vera weren't due back for at least a couple of hours. Peering over my shoulder, I was stunned to see the tall, and dashing, David Dean standing there with a tray of coffees and a bag of goodies.

I slipped the headphone off one ear.

"Ah, good morning." A tinge of surprise coloured my words. Of all people, this was not who I expected to see today.

"I hope you don't mind, but I brought you a little something." He lifted the Sylvia's Bakery bag, which was spotted with grease marks. Whatever was inside was most likely tasty and the very idea of a mouth-watering pastry made my stomach growl.

Removing my headset, I rested it on my shoulders.

"What did I do to receive this unexpected surprise?"

I hadn't given him my home address so he could pop in all willy-nilly when the mood struck. This was my personal space, but I tried to keep my tone in check.

"Well, the thing is, when I went to get my coffee and danish, the lady at the bakery doubled up the order, and since I was passing by, I figured I'd drop one off with you."

Likely story. I was on the edge of town, Sylvia's Bakery was on Main Street in the downtown core. He actually would've had to backtrack to come past my place, but still, the sentiment was sweet. Probably ordered double. Maybe. Or maybe Libby was working. That girl was always up to something.

Stepping on the scattered sawdust and shavings, I made my way over to him. "Thank you. That's very kind to think of me."

The smile stretching across his face was a mile wide. He read the labels on the side of the takeaway cups. "Do you prefer a Chai Latte or a Mochaccino?"

"I'd love the Chai, please. I like a little spice."

"Do you?" A charming laugh rolled out as he handed me the tea.

Slightly embarrassed that he read more into my words than I had intended, I shook my head and ran down a list of possible topics to deflect to.

"Okay, I have to ask. How do you know sign language?"

He straightened to his full height. "My cousin is completely deaf and has been all his life. It was just something I grew up knowing."

"Wow, that's really neat. Not many people in this town know ASL. Vera can hear, but it's awful, at least according to the audiologist. It's more like hearing someone scream underwater unless she's wearing her hearing aid, but that can only do so much."

"Has she had hearing loss long?"

"She was diagnosed a few years back. Within the next couple of years though, she'll be completely deaf." A silent world I couldn't possibly imagine.

"That's got to be rough. For the both of you."

Since we needed a clear space to set the bag and tray down, I quickly grabbed a cloth and dusted off a corner of the makeshift desk I'd propped up. "We're managing though. My work helps to pay those bills."

He set the items down and smoothed out a napkin before pulling out the two danishes. Both were chocolate, and with the slight sheen on the dark chocolate, they were still warm. My saliva glands fired up, and I hadn't even had a bite yet.

"Have you started the mural pieces yet?" He pressed the drink to his lips.

I took a dainty nibble and sighed. It was heavenly. Even with Libby's discount, I didn't order these often, so this was a real treat.

"I haven't yet." I pointed to the corner where the long boards were set up in a haphazard order. "But I have all the pieces. I should be able to start soon though. Once school is back in, I'll have more uninterrupted time to work. Until then, I've been making the cutouts for the booth pieces. Want to see?"

"Yes, please." He took a quick sip and set his mochaccino on the edge of the napkin after wiping his lips. His full, perfectly rose-coloured lips.

Good lord, I needed help.

Over in the area I'd designated as the David zone, since I had a myriad of pieces on the go, I stacked together the layers to give him a rough idea. Once I had them all cut, I needed to carve and add in the details, but at least he could get a sense of what was being worked on.

"You like?"

"Very much." His eyes danced across the one piece I held tightly in my grip, scanning the area until he met my eyes. "I can see the beauty within."

I knew it wasn't directed at me personally, but to the artwork, however, it made my heart rate jump a notch and my breath caught in my throat.

Swallowing to wet my dry as a desert mouth, I whispered, "Thank you."

I turned away and set the boards on the table, pointing out where I'd planned on adding depth and designs to morph the plain wood into something beautiful.

As I lifted one of the layers, it slipped out of my hand, and both David and I caught it at the same time.

"Thanks." His hand cradled mine, all warm and soft, unlike my rough and calloused hands. Thank goodness he was only touching the top.

Pulsating currents of heated electricity shot up my arm, and I chanced a gaze into his eyes. He held me there for several heartbeats before he cleared his throat and backed away.

It was the most sensual moment I'd had since, well, it had been a long time. Guys didn't date pregnant women, they didn't date single mothers with a newborn, and they sure as hell didn't date a woman with a toddler. Once that pregnancy stick popped up with two lines, my future dates were already written off.

Hands shaking from the most contact I'd had in years, I set the layer back on the table. "I'm glad you like it. How are the renovations going?"

"On schedule, thank Christ."

"Oh?"

"I hate renovations. Everything is a mess, everything in disarray, and you can never find what you're looking for when you need it."

"Like a metamorphosis."

He pointed at me with a smile on his face. "Exactly. I like that."

"From the caterpillar emerges a butterfly, different in so many ways, yet still the same on the inside, just better and stronger."

"Sounds like you speak from experience?" His brow lifted with the question, and he took a bite of his pastry.

"Oh no, I am no butterfly, and I am still fully ensconced in my cocoon. My metamorphosis is so far from complete, it's not even close." I dusted off a stool for David, and then took a seat at my desk. "Please."

"I really can't stay. I just wanted to check on things."

"Do you do this with your staff too?" The taste of the spices from the tea was invigorating.

"What's that? Bring them treats?" He lifted the danish into the air.

"No, the micromanaging."

He chuckled and straightened himself up. "Is that what you think I'm doing?"

I playfully shrugged and kept my focus on him. "Maybe?"

"I don't micromanage."

I cocked an eyebrow, wishing it looked as cute as Libby when she did it. It was hard to take her seriously when it popped onto her face.

"Fine, maybe I do it a little."

"Admitting it is the first step. Congratulations."

He nearly spit out his drink with his laugh. "You're funny."

"Not really, I just happen to have a tendency to say what's on my mind."

"You have no idea how refreshing that is."

"Really now? I thought men loved it when girls played dumb, curled their hair around their fingers while batting their long, fake lashes, and say whatever a man wants to hear." I attempted to flirt with my eyes, but the speed necessary was giving me a headache.

He snorted and stepped closer. "Maybe some guys, but I am not one of those." He turned all serious, and somehow the intensity forming on his face was intriguing rather than threatening. "You want the truth?"

"Always."

"I came here today to see if you…" A sharp inhale cut through the space. "Would you like to go out with me?"

Chapter Nine

Gobsmacked was the best word I could come up with, and my stuttered response wasn't much better.

"Really? Me?"

"Is there someone else here I'm not seeing?" It was cute how he stared, how the edges of his eyes crinkled with a hint of a grin, and how sexy and alluring he looked.

What the hell was wrong with me? This man nearly cost me everything years ago, and now he was trying to charm me, and successfully I might add.

"Well, I…"

"Oh shit, I never thought to ask." He pulled back and his grin stretched into a grimace. "Maybe you are seeing someone else, and I totally misread all the vibes."

Oh my god, there were vibes? What kind of signals was I putting off?

"Ah, no, there's no one else. I'm a single mother. That's the best dating repellant you can buy." I laughed at my own words but stopped when he didn't return the gesture.

"That should have zero effect on things."

"But it does. Having a child, on my own, immediately kicked me out of the dating pool." I dropped my focus to the grease-stained napkin in front of me, although I wasn't ashamed of my daughter, quite the opposite. "I'm okay with that. Vera means everything to me, and she's my world."

"I admire that." He tipped up my chin. "I think single motherhood is amazing."

I swallowed. "You do?"

"You're so strong and capable, and you don't need anyone's help. The reason you think guys might not be interested in you isn't because you have a child, it's because your strength and independence are wholly intimidating to them. It makes us the weaker sex, which…" He leaned closer and lowered his voice to a deep, throaty sound. "We are but don't like to admit that."

A heat forged deep between my thighs. What the actual hell?

He cleared his throat and put a little cooling distance between us. "So, now that we've established how your single motherhood is not a deterrent, and you don't have a boyfriend or husband lurking around ready to pound me for asking, what do you say to a date?"

"When?" I swallowed. That one-word answer alone told me all I felt in my soul. Despite who he was, I was strangely attracted to him and I wanted to go out with him, maybe even see if sex with a partner was still the same, or different, or better.

"I'm flexible, but now that I know you're interested…" He circled my heated face and tapped me gently on the nose. "Is it alright if I plan something fun?"

"I like fun." My words withered as I spoke, and I suddenly felt like I was sixteen all over again and the cute guy from the baseball team was asking me out.

"Perfect. I'll call you soon with the details." He popped the last bite of his pastry into his mouth.

"I do need a bit of heads-up since I need to secure a babysitter."

"I can arrange that."

I shook my head. "No, no, no. I have two sitters I use as I don't trust anyone else."

The corner of his mouth pushed up. "Oh, I get that, and I completely understand. I meant I can arrange the date with some lead time."

I was an idiot. Of course, that's what he meant. "Thank you."

"Call you soon?"

"I look forward to it."

He stepped to the door and the chimes rang.

"Thank you for the treat. I appreciate it." I called out before he walked out of view.

"My pleasure."

He disappeared, and suddenly I was in dire need of a shower, the colder the better. That man had somehow stirred the embers deep inside. I never thought they'd ever be warmed enough to flick back to life.

Wanting to see David again, and with no solid reasoning for it, two days later I popped in unannounced to Birch Bay Burgers. It was still strange being in the restaurant, but I found myself laughing a little too, which helped reduce a little of the tension lodged into a tight ball in my gut. I'd been a visitor more times in the past couple of weeks than I had in the last seven years.

A section of the place was tarped with polyfilm, obstructing the ocean view beyond. Likely did a better job of killing his business than I ever had. At least half the space was unusable.

However, it was lunchtime, and the place was packed. So maybe it had the opposite effect and people clamored in at all hours to eat here.

"Can I help you?" The hostess asked, blowing a section of her perfectly spiraled ringlets away from her face.

"Oh, no thanks. I'm just waiting for someone."

She turned and swaggered away, and I continued to scan the place. Across the dining room, I spotted David, looking as handsome as ever.

He stopped at a table and was having a conversation with the diners, and then lowered himself to the same level as the little guy swinging his legs.

My heart warmed at the gesture.

David rose and shook the hand of the guest as he nodded, turning toward me. His face lit up with the kind of smile I'd thought I'd never have a guy give me.

He walked in my direction, stopping briefly to say hello to the other tables. "Good morning, Erin. To what do I owe this absolute pleasure?"

The way his eyes raked over me filled me with joy. I had purposely picked a top that was a little more ladylike than my typical wear, and I paired it with dark capris. I even took more than two minutes with my hair.

Francesca did not miss the effort involved and sent me on my way with a wave and a whispering of *good luck*.

"I wanted to show you a part of the artwork." I squared my shoulders and pushed out my chest. Just a little. Not enough to be considered hardcore or anything.

"I'd love to see. Let's go to my office."

"Lead the way."

That was the best view. Or at least one of them. Seeing his tight behind in those form-fitting dress pants was a huge turn-on. Maybe I could get a little *happy-happy-joy-joy* out of him before the mural was finished. Did they even call it that anymore?

We walked into the kitchen, lit up brighter than an operating room. The stainless steel stations reflected the brightness, and I was a little surprised no one was wearing sunglasses. However, as I gazed around while sticking the length of the wall, there wasn't a mess to be found. Every flat area and countertop was dazzling, aside from the plates of food in process of being created.

One chef was lifting a lid, and with his bare fingers, pulled off a stainless steel lid and retrieved a perfect piece of lettuce which he placed on a white plate.

"Erin?"

"Oh, sorry." I followed him over to a curving staircase.

Just beyond that was a sign stating employees must wash their hands for one minute before returning to their stations. Well, at least there was that. David obviously took cleanliness seriously *now*, as I was sure doctors and nurses scrubbed for two minutes, according to the latest Grey's Anatomy episode.

The top of the stairwell opened to a bright office, lit up by the overhead lights similar to the kitchen's, which overlooked the bay, with tiny windows along the floor providing a view of the dining room. To the far side, there were floor-to-ceiling windows and the kitchen spread out below with a bustling crew working on the lunch rush. He had his eye on everything from this vantage point. Definitely took the micromanaging term to a whole new level.

"Wow, this is some space." It wasn't huge by any stretch, maybe a couple of booths wide, but with all the surrounding windows, it appeared quite spacious.

"The windows are all one-way. I can see into the kitchen and out into the dining room if I sit here." He sat at his desk, which was meticulous. Not a stray pen resting on the keyboard, not a lone paperclip to be seen. Pretty sure there wasn't even a speck of dust on the monitor.

"Impressive." But it was more than just the space, it was him too. Some of the hatred I'd had for this man was rubbing away with each minute I spent in his presence.

"You wanted to show me something?"

Did I ever. As much as I'd once fantasized about wiping away a desktop and making sweet love on top of it, it was just a pipe dream. This was reality.

I inhaled and pulled out my phone. "I wanted to show you—" Tapping on the image of one of his booth pieces, I pointed to a small detail. "This."

He tipped his head to look closer. "Is that a butterfly?"

"It's little." I lifted my hand and pinched out an inch. "But after our conversations, especially the part about the transformation, I thought I'd add in a little bonus. Something maybe only you would get, but still. One of those hidden image things."

"I love it." He couldn't take his eyes off the image. "There's so much detail."

"Not really. It was fun, and only took an hour." It was a time killer while I waited for inspiration to hit.

He tore his gaze away from my phone as he handed it back.

Rocking in his chair, he thoughtfully rubbed his chin. "Can you add one to each piece?"

"Absolutely."

"I'll pay you extra for your time."

"No, this was on me. I don't mind. I wasn't sure if it would work, and turns out, it did." I tried to hide my smile with a nonchalant shrug.

"You really have a talent."

Did he say these things just to see if I'd blush? Because it worked, every single time. I was going to be putty in his hands if he didn't stop and if I didn't let the comments just bounce off me. They were just words, and he could be saying them just to say them.

My breath shuddered. "Thank you."

He rose and looked into the kitchen; a frown formed turning his grin upside down. "Just a second, please."

Without a word, he descended the staircase and marched over to one of the stainless-steel workstations. He pointed and the worker bristled slightly but nodded in agreement with whatever was being said. A moment later, shoulders down, David stepped away and his footsteps grew louder as he ascended into the office.

He ran his hands over his reddened face. "Sorry about that."

I shook my head. "No worries. We're at your place of work, you're entitled to micromanage your staff." I grinned at the same time as he did.

"This was beyond micromanaging. He messed up, and it was

caught before it escalated into a nightmare."

My jovial tone fell like a rock in the water. "Trust me, it's all good. I'm just ribbing you."

I tossed my phone into my purse and shifted back and forth on my feet.

He glanced quickly into the kitchen area and nodded, before returning his attention to me. "Since you're here and before I forget, I have a date prepared."

My heart hammered in anticipation.

"How flexible are you with dates and times?"

"Marginally. Depends on Francesca's availability."

This upcoming weekend was her last shift at the Cowboy Den, so if David had something planned, I'd need to reach out to Adam, or if Mia wasn't busy then her.

"Sunday? Does that work?"

Guess I'd be asking Adam or Mia. I laughed to myself. "Let me check with my family, and I'll get back to you."

He cleared his throat and his Adam's Apple bobbed. "I await your reply."

I held my breath and took in his handsome face. "I'll stop by the store on my way home and let you know."

"May I have the kitchen make you a lunch before you go?"

"As sweet as that is, no, no thank you. I didn't come for lunch." And after the scene I'd just witnessed, it's best to avoid eating. Not sure what he saw. "Just wanted to show you the butterfly." I lingered at the doorway, my body begging me to stay, but my head telling me it was time to go – anticipation heightening the pleasure and all that.

"I'll walk you down."

I took my time descending to the main floor but rushed through the kitchen. It was like watching a ballet – the performers all moving in synchronicity – and I didn't want to mess anything up by standing there and being in the way.

At the hostess stand, I stopped and turned.

David was right there, a deepening desire on his face. "Talk soon."

"Soon."

I had to force myself to go, and once I was out the door, I raced to my car and over to the bookshop. Adam had better not have any plans.

Chapter Ten

Since our date was scheduled for a Sunday afternoon, and Francesca was still nursing a hangover from her final night at the Cowboy Den, I dropped Vera off at Adam's place with a kiss on her forehead. Unsure of what to wear, and having no idea what the mystery date included, I chose to wear simple black pants and a loose striped top that I hoped would make me look thinner than I was. I also brought a sweater, just in case we were out into the evening hours. This way, I was prepared for everything.

Right on time, David pulled in front of the bookstore in his Mini Cooper and exited to meet me on the sidewalk. I'd had the foresight to be watching out the window, waiting in anticipation, so it was easy to walk as nonchalantly as possible outside.

"You look amazing, Erin."

It never failed to put a smile on my face, a sizzle in my cheeks, and a spring in my step. "Thank you. You do as well."

Although I'd only seen him in dress pants and a buttoned top – every single time – there was no doubt David could make grey sweatpants and a ripped tee look impressive. Even on a Sunday afternoon, he was dressed nicely.

"So where are we off to?" I asked, curiosity ripe in my words.

"Well, I've been giving that a lot of thought and weight. After our conversation in your workshop, I wanted to do something for you that would be memorable. You've said you don't go out on many dates…"

Thank goodness that's what he heard, although it's not what I said. *Many* dates was a giant stretch.

"And I wondered, what could I do to make this special for you?"

As sweet as that was, I had to open my mouth. "Just do what you do with your other dates."

He laughed and covered his heart with his hand.

"Why? What do you normally do?" I leaned forward as I lowered my voice.

"Honestly?"

"Yeah?"

"I take them out for dinner and then take them back to my place."

"Oh."

So, he was a deeply skilled lover, light years ahead of me. Even if I wanted to bed the man, I'd be so out of practice it would be laughable. I vowed to not let things get that far, but maybe that was his plan being a Sunday afternoon date. Maybe he knew I wasn't sex material, just afternoon fun. Suddenly my spirit was crushed by the weight of my heavy thoughts.

"And I think you deserve a little more respect than that."

"I'm flattered. Is it because I'm a single mom?" I looked beyond him to the busy main street where pedestrians walked in groups, laughing and having fun.

"It's because I get the idea you don't treat yourself much. You put Vera's needs ahead of your own."

While it was true – because didn't every mother? – I was shocked he'd picked up on that. "How could you know that after only seeing me a few times?"

"I saw the state of your house, and the clothes you wear, and yet when I met Vera, she was in ironed clothing, with her hair done, and didn't look like she had any needs unattended."

I flashed back to my own messy hair – my signature two-minute style, if it even took that long.

"But it's more than that. I watched you interact with her, and it was easy to see the love you have for her."

"Wow – you're quite observant."

This time, he blushed. "Maybe. Or maybe it was the way your eyes rolled back in your head when you had a bite of an ordinary chocolate danish."

"Okay, those are just heavenly." I tipped my head in a

knowing way.

He shrugged. "My point is, you deserve more than a little wining and dining."

Well, now my curiosity was highly piqued. "So what do you have planned?"

"I've ruled out anything loud and noisy that precludes us from having a conversation, because I want to get to know all about you, so I hope you don't mind, but I thought we'd go berry picking and then we could go back to my place and bake a pie."

"Are you serious?" I wanted to laugh, but not at the idea because that actually sounded wonderful.

"Yeah, why?" His expression was as confused as could be.

"When you said you normally take your dates back home, I thought it was for sex, not to bake pies."

With that, he chuckled. "Ah, yes. Well, there is truth in that. Ninety percent of the time, we do go back for that specific reason, but never to bake a pie."

"Ah, I see. Well, at least you admit to being a player."

"A player? On come on, I'm better than that."

I cocked an eyebrow.

"Okay, fine. But I wanted to try something different with you. You seem—"

"Different?" I tossed the pitiful word out.

"No, better. Like I need to put you on a higher standard than the others."

"That's weird. I'm no different than they are."

He gently bumped my hand. "And that's what makes you special. The others, they all think they are better than everyone else."

I broke eye contact and turned my head. A light breeze pushed a piece of garbage down the street.

"So, berry picking and pie making? You up for it?"

Colour me happy. "Hell yeah. But I should warn you, it's been a while since I've made pie dough."

"Then you're a step ahead of me as I never have." He opened the car door for me. "I don't want to keep you away from your daughter for too long, so shall we go?"

I slipped into the seat and chanced a glance to Adam's apartment above the bookstore. Instantly, the curtains swung shut.

I covered my mouth with my hand and nosed toward the building. "Adam was watching."

David turned around and cupped his mouth. "I promise to take good care of her."

No doubt, Adam was cringing. Not only was he visually busted, but he was also called out on it too.

David winked as his smile grew wider. He sauntered to his side of the car and dropped into the driver's seat.

"Where's this berry farm?"

"You've lived here all your life, right?"

I nodded. Never felt the urge to be anywhere else.

"Ever hear of Magpie Lake?"

"That's on the other side of the strait, isn't it?"

"It sure is." He put the car into drive, and we pulled away from the bookstore. "Music?"

"Sure, why not? What's on your playlist?"

One of my friends actually dumped a guy because he was into country music, and she was a heavy metal fan. Not sure it would be a make-it-or-break-it deal for me, but it did pique my interest into what music David liked.

"I'm a sucker for 70s classics."

"Zepplin?"

"Queen, truth be told."

"Oh my god, I love them. They're on my playlist for when I'm in the shop. *Somebody to Love* is one of my favourite songs."

With a couple taps on his phone, the song started playing, and I was relaxing in my seat, mumbling along to the words. Another couple of songs played through, and then the opening words of one of their most popular songs.

"May I?" My hand hovered over the volume knob.

"Please do."

I cranked it up and started singing along. This was the perfect car song, and as I hoped would happen, David started singing along too. He was as tone-deaf as I was, but we were bobbing our heads to the beat as we pulled into the U-Pick farm, and we sat in the car, bleating out the music like we were at a karaoke bar.

Then the song ended, and David killed the engine.

"Well, that was fun." My two feet hit the ground with a renewed sense of energy.

"I've never done that before."

"Really? Not with your wife? Or bestie?"

He shook his head.

"Maybe it's a good thing you're divorced then." I nudged him playfully. "Because if that song comes on and you don't sing along, then…" But I stopped myself. I wasn't going to add the rest of the sentence *you shouldn't be together* because that wasn't fair.

I tossed my gaze to the ground.

"I get it. Trust me, I get it." There was a slight grin stretching out, but it was the light in his eyes that soothed me. "That was fun." He pointed to the little white shed at the entrance to the farm. "Shall we go pick some berries?"

Two hours later, we parked in David's garage and hauled in four buckets of our fresh pickings; blueberries, raspberries, huckleberries, and cherries.

David's kitchen was immaculate and had a very institutional feel. Aside from neatly arranged mixing bowls, measuring cups, and ingredients, his countertops were devoid of items. Not a coffee maker. Or a container of utensils. It was such a minimalist-looking approach I was terrified the berry juice would somehow stain his marble countertops.

He set a bucket in each sink. "What kind of pie should we make?"

I scanned for a safe place to set my buckets down, walking around the island in search of someplace suitable.

David brushed my hand with his, as he'd done all afternoon, while he grabbed my buckets and added them to the sink.

"We can make a mixed berry pie," I said to his question.

"Do you know the ratios?"

"A little of each?" I shrugged. "It was how my grandma did it and her pies were always amazing."

David started running the water, but I didn't miss the slight cringe with my less-than-precise roundabout way of adding the filling. "Okay, if that's how you've done it previously."

"It'll be fine, I promise. Can I help?" I stood beside him. "There's so many berries."

Washing them all was going to take hours.

"We'll measure out what you think you need and wash those up. The rest I can do later."

Together, we scooped out what I thought was the appropriate amount, stopping once in a while to taste a berry, although I swore I was going to burst from the sampling we'd done all afternoon. The raspberries were highly addictive and sweet with just the right amount of tartness. Grandma would've been happy with these.

Our hands bumped together as we froze them under the cool water rinse, and there were many heartbeats of steady eye contact.

Drying off the berries on a phenomenal amount of slowly turning pink paper towels, we set them aside as we stood on either side of the counter.

David quickly tossed them into the garbage before I had a chance of reusing them.

"Wasn't sure which kind you'd need." He pointed to the three small bags of flour and read out the ingredient list as I pulled the bag of white flour toward me. It was petite-sized; it wouldn't last a month in our house.

"Food processor?" I searched. David shook his head. "No problem, I'll freeze up some forks. Those would be?"

"Drawer beside the fridge. Third space from the left."

And what a drawer. I didn't know they made organizers with so many spots. Dessert forks, dinner forks, small spoons, large spoons, knives, and spots for the can opener, several other items I wasn't sure of their purpose, but they each had a place in his perfectly arranged drawer.

After throwing a couple of forks into the freezer, I grabbed the measuring cups off the counter and unhooked the bottom one. "You've never made a pie before, right?"

"No."

"Then I think it's high time you got messy and learned." I winked. "Best way to learn is by doing."

"That's why you're here though. I'll watch you mix it all together." He pulled up a stool and sat at the counter.

"I ain't no Henny Penny."

"Hey," he scoffed and leaned on the counter, narrowing the distance between us. "I helped pick berries."

"Yes, you did." And how much fun was that? Who knew? "However, you're going to dig in, and I'm going to show you how much fun baking can be."

"Do you bake a lot?"

"Sometimes Vera and I will make muffins, but as a rule, I'll whip them together while she's in school or at camp. She has dietary restrictions, so I'm a wee bit of a worrier when it comes to her food."

"I'll send you home with a bucket of berries then."

"Oh, no. You don't have to do that."

"They'll go bad here."

I shook my head. "Freeze them on a parchment-lined cookie sheet and put them into a Ziploc when they're frozen."

"Really?"

I set the measuring cup down. "Seriously? You didn't know that?"

"I've never had to do this."

Yeah, he didn't strike me as a guy who knew his way around a kitchen, not in his own home anyway, and overseeing what his staff were doing wasn't the same.

"Well then, it's high time you learned."

I grabbed an apron off the back of the pantry door and walked over to him, fastening it to his body. Slowly tying the straps together

109

while checking out the build of his shoulders and inhaling the light cologne fragrance. For good measure, I tapped his back when I was done, and released my breath.

"All done?" There was a playfulness on the tip of his tongue which was going to be my undoing if I didn't watch myself.

"Yup." Calming the race of my quickened heartbeat, I walked back over to my side. "Add your dry ingredients into a sieve first. Do you have one of those?"

"Yes," he said and pointed to the pantry.

I opened the well-organized space, shocked at the labeling and detail. All cans were facing label side out, and all boxes were divided into proper groups of pasta, cereal, and crackers. Mine, by contrast, was wherever there was room, that's where it went. Finding the metal sieve was an easy task, and I stepped back out with it in my hand.

"Where did you learn to be so—"

"Organized?" He questioned with a mile-high cocked eyebrow.

"High-maintenance? That, in there, is over the top, although I am more than a tad jealous. One look and you know exactly what you needed versus my wild guess." I bet his grocery lists were likely well-detailed and organized by aisle too.

"For some. I can't function without order." It was said so matter-of-factly, it had me wondering if he'd always been that way, or if something had happened to warrant that level of organization.

"Well, I'll be thorough in my teachings." I winked.

"I hope so." A twinkle appeared in his eyes.

"Okay. Let's begin. Measure out the flour and pour it into this." I put the sieve over a bowl.

Cup by cup he measured it out, making it precise as he dragged his knife over the top of the measuring cup, his tongue sticking out just a little with concentration. He added it to the sieve, along with the other dry ingredients, and went to shake it.

"Gently," I said, covering his hand with mine to slow his rhythm. "These things must be done delicately."

He stared into my eyes, making my heartbeat peak faster than any cardio workout. "I can take it slow."

I swallowed. Never in my life had baking been such a turn-on. Mind you, I'd never baked with a man before, not even with my brothers or father.

With the dry ingredients mixed, I pulled out the two frozen forks. "Now we're going to incorporate the butter into the flour."

"You mean mix?"

"Nope. You want to cut the butter into the mixture. It'll resemble a coarse cornmeal." I added the slices of butter into the mix and demonstrated. "Now you."

The muscles on his forearm tightened with each downward push of the fork, and it was riveting to watch him concentrate on adding the butter without actually mixing. Once again, the tip of his tongue snuck out between his perfectly plump lips.

"That look okay?"

I broke my stare from his arms and focused on the flour mixture. It was crumbly and lumpy. "It's perfect. Now you keep doing that, while I add the water."

As he *mixed* I added the ice-cold water, a tablespoon at a time, explaining why it needed to be so cold. He was an attentive student and took in every syllable I spoke.

The mixture was perfect and ready for chilling before rolling. It seemed the dough and I had something in common.

After wrapping and tossing it in the freezer, I stood in front of his fridge. "Now we wait before rolling it out." I stared into the depths of his eyes. "What should we do in the meantime?

A million little possibilities existed. A further tour of his house. A stop at the bedroom. A romp in his bed. I licked my lips, hoping for a little subtlety.

"We could make the filling?"

As if wrapped in smoke and blown away, my desire blew with it. "Good idea."

The player in him clearly wasn't interested in me, and with that realization, my heart shrunk.

Chapter Eleven

ibby handed me a steaming cup of coffee while I curled up on my worn-out, once-loved sofa; she always made the best homemade version of a latte, so I gave her free roam in my kitchen. "So, let me get this straight, you went berry picking and back to his place to bake a pie, and he didn't so much as give you a goodbye, knee-weakening, foot tossed in the air kind of kiss?"

I shook my head and stared into the cup, watching as the little bubbles in the frothy milk popped one by one. "I did get a quick kiss on the cheek."

"That doesn't count."

It did in my books. It was more than I'd had since Vera was born, but it had been a year before Vera's father since I'd had a really good kiss; the exact kind Libby had just described. The kind that leaves you breathless too.

"And you wanted more?"

"At least try it out. It's been a while." I took a quick sip – the foam was sweet with a hint of caramel.

"I can't believe he blew you off. Bastard." Libby tugged up her thigh-high stockings before she sat down, curling her long legs underneath. Today she wore bright purple with her white skirt. "You're so sweet and amazing, so he's the idiot for not making a move. Something must be wrong with him." Her voice started to pitch. "You know, I have half a mind to storm over to Birch Bay and say a few things."

I covered her hand. "Don't. I'm not worth it."

Apparently.

He wasn't interested, even if he was putting out the signs. Or was I just reading way too much into it? First guy to look at me in years, not as a mother or a woodcarver, but as someone else, and naturally, I fell for the charms and was ready to bed the guy. Seriously, how embarrassing. I was a grown woman, a mother for crying out loud, I shouldn't have acted like a desperate, horny teenager.

"You are worth it, and if he can't see that—"

"Then it's on him?" I got that, but they were just words.

Everyone said those exact words. Adam was the forerunner on that, with Mia and Francesca battling it out for second, although Fran never had a problem securing a date to anything. She was frustratingly perfect in looks, charm, and her desire to do things her own way. A fantastic role model for Vera. Mia was too. Both were the sunshine to my rain clouds.

"It is. I know you don't believe me."

"It's really hard to when I haven't had a date in years. Years, Libby. Not since before Vera. Single motherhood is a bonafide date killer. *Oh hey, I think I like you. What's that? You have a child? Oh, I, well, I only said I liked you, I'm not interested in an insta-family.*"

One guy, who I thought had been interested in me, did a complete one-eighty when he learned I had a child and said he was too young to think about a family. Too young? He was twenty-eight, not eighteen. We'd gone out once, and I hadn't even considered a second date, let alone make him part of the family before he dropped that bombshell on me.

"Then honestly, he isn't the right guy. He should be wowed by your independence not repelled by it."

I set my coffee down on the table, trying to match it up with the heat-stained ring. "It is what it is. However, David's also my client, and I'm working on a big project for him, with a big payback."

"How much extra did you charge him?" She leaned forward.

"Not as much as you wanted, but enough to give me, well Vera and I, a nice cushion." It would help take a bit of pressure off the long winter months when I needed to rely more on internet sales than markets.

Plus, winter was coming and the tires on my truck were quite bald. With the new incoming cash, the possibility existed of getting newer takeoffs with more tread, rather than the ones with only 40%

remaining. Or I could address the slow leak in the roof. Or set some money aside for Vera's next hearing aid.

Libby spoke, pulling me away from the running list of needs to take care of. "Way to go. I'm glad you charged him a little more."

There was pride in her words I took to heart, but it also came with a side of guilt. When I created the contract, I was still angry with him, but since getting to know him better, he'd turned out to be a nice guy. Maybe I could add in a little something extra, to help alleviate some of the guilt. Besides, it's not like he'd ever find out about the price adjustment. There's just no way that would ever happen.

A vehicle pulled into the driveway, and I peeked from behind the gauzy curtains. A little Mini. Didn't the guy ever stop checking in on me?

"Well, he's here." My voice dropped.

"David?"

I closed the curtains and fell back onto the sofa. "Yep. In addition to blowing me off, he's also a micromanager. Bet he's here to look at what I've accomplished so far with his pieces. Truth be told, at this rate, I'll be happy when it's done." Especially since nothing in the romance department will ever happen; the last date was proof of that. "I could pretend I'm not home. I'm allowed, right?"

She nodded and kept quiet as the doorbell rang.

"Ah, fuck it. Let me show him what I've done, and I'll be right back." I rose and headed for the back door.

Libby was hot on my heels, chuckling and whispering as if David was already in the house. "You think that's what he's doing? Checking on you?"

"I know it is."

"You are so wrong. He's inventing an excuse to see you." She jumped in front of me and crossed her arms over her chest. "Maybe he's more into you than you think."

"That's not it." I was shaking my head rapidly.

"How many times has he just—"

A knock came from the back door.

"I need to get this." I walked through my kitchen, down the four stairs to the back door, and pulled it open. My jaw hit the floor.

On the other side was a giant bouquet, and hidden just behind it, was David. "These are for you."

"Oh wow, thanks." The bottom was a box with handles to hold the large arrangement.

He poked his head out from the side. "I had them include a vase, just in case."

"Thank you." I took the heavy bouquet from him, touching his hands briefly as I did. Despite the lack of intimacy the other day, but a whole lot of what I thought was chemistry, my body was still involuntarily reacting to him in a very carnal way.

I stood there as a debate settled in. Did I invite him in? Did I show him the pieces? I wasn't sure what I was supposed to do.

Leave it to Libby to figure it out. "We were just having

coffee. Let me get you one. How do you like it, David?"

"Who's that?" He whispered, as his gaze flew up the landing where Libby had disappeared from sight.

Damn.

"That's my friend, Libby. She works at Sylvia's Bakery." I stepped back on the landing. "Why don't you come in?"

He hesitated for a heartbeat. "Sure, but I can't stay long. I didn't come to impose. I just wanted to make sure I dropped off the flowers in person. You never know if or when these teenage drivers will actually make a delivery. However, I have time for a quick coffee, but I need to be at the restaurant before it opens in an hour."

"Isn't someone there already to start getting things ready?"

Of course, while it was laced with sarcasm, I hadn't been playful enough in my tone, and his brows knit together as his eyes narrowed slightly.

He picked at the edge of his beard, but followed it up with a wink. "Yes, my floor manager is there, but, as you know, I like to micromanage, so I need to be there too. Make sure they are doing it correctly."

"Sorry, that was a dumb thing to have asked."

"It's all good." At least he chuckled when he spoke, although the soft nudge against my forearm was enough to fire up the girlish giggles inside me.

"Please, don't linger and come in."

We walked up the stairs and into the kitchen. Libby was

refilling the pod for the machine.

"How do you like your coffee?"

"Libby, is it?"

"That's right. You're the owner of the Birch Bay Burgers, and you've taken my friend out on a fun berry-picking and pie-making date." The way she said it, it sounded like I shared every detail with her about David, which wasn't true. She didn't know he was divorced.

"You're a regular at the restaurant?" He stood by my 1950's style table, placing his hands on the back of a metal-edged, vinyl-padded chair.

"Not anymore." She turned away. "I live at the bakery, so when I'm not there, I'm not really anywhere. Except here, once in a while."

David mouthed the words *not anymore.*

I thought I'd die a little. Libby was always painfully honest, but this was a moment that could call for a little white lie and no one would be the wiser. She used to visit Birch Bay Burgers, until I shared my personal tale with her.

Libby bounced around the counter, as I stood there, unable to articulate my thoughts. "How do you take your coffee? You haven't really said."

David shrugged and sent a quick look in my direction. "I'm not picky. Black? With cream? Really, whatever is easiest."

She opened my fridge and pulled out the homogenized milk.

119

"She makes a mean cup of coffee, you're sure to enjoy it." I set my sights on David, but it was really hard to not watch Libby jump around.

"Interesting. I may need to hire you at the restaurant." David let out a soft laugh.

"You can't afford me."

"Libby." My eyes widened.

However, David countered well. "Knowing Sylvia as well as I do, no doubt she pays top dollar. She treats her staff well, am I right?"

She only nodded, and I thought he was a little caught off guard as she tipped her head to the side.

I set the box of flowers on the counter and inhaled the sweet, addictive scent. Between the carnations and roses and lilies, it was borderline assault, but in the best possible way.

"These are really gorgeous, thank you." I pulled the flowers and vase from the box, nose deep between the stems once again, and set it in the middle of my white table, the bright colours popping on display.

"I saw them and thought of you."

Libby put her hands over her heart and made an *aww* face. Thank goodness she was behind David, and he didn't witness her display.

"Are you here to see your work?"

"Nope. Just wanted to drop these off and see how your day

was going so far." He took the coffee Libby had made and took a sip. "This is good, real good."

"Thank you." She disappeared into the living room and returned with our mugs.

I stood on one side of the peninsula, beside Libby, and across from David. No one spoke, just the occasional slurp or squeak following a sip of coffee.

He cleared his throat and stared into his cup before lifting his gaze to meet my eyes. "I know Saturday is a market day for you, but do you have plans that evening?"

I shifted back and forth on my feet, trying not to look at Libby. No doubt she wore a wild-eyed smile. "I'm pretty sure my social calendar is wide open. Vera and I were maybe going to have a picnic on the beach, but that's about all."

"Oh well, I don't want to take time away from your daughter." His words almost backtracked like he was doing, putting some distance between him and the counter.

I raced to think fast before he pulled the invite away. "It's all good. Saturdays are typically quite busy anyway. Vera and I can go Friday night or Sunday night. The beach will still be there, and the weather is likely better those days too."

Libby pulled her phone out and thumbed through a few open apps. "Yep. Friday night looks like an all-star night for picnics on the beach."

"There you go." How desperate was I suddenly sounding? I

needed to cool things off a bit. Desperation was a smell I didn't want to give off.

"Perfect. So… Saturday night, it's a date?"

A date. The words sang in the air, and I may have been the one to put the high notes on top.

David drank his coffee, his gaze flitting from me to Libby and back again. "Can I pick you up?"

"Sure. What will we be doing?"

"Are you opposed to seafood? I know you have some kind of chicken hatred."

"It's not a hatred per se, but no, I don't have seafood allergies." Just that seafood was typically allergic to my pay, as in there wasn't enough money for it.

"And you are okay with dressing up for the evening?"

Colour me intrigued and Libby too, as her face brightened as if the clouds had just parted, highlighting her in a ray of sunshine.

"How fancy?" I internally cringed at the idea of needing a ball gown, although the thought of David in a tuxedo produced a lot of great mental images.

"Business fancy?"

That was a new one, and I laughed accordingly. "What level is that?"

"A nice outfit. Not black tie, but maybe something you'd wear to a wedding."

"A wedding, eh? We're not going to one, are we?"

"Oh god, no."

"Whew. I'm sure I can find something suitable and *business fancy*." My selection wasn't great but there was a secondhand store in Stewart Surf I could go browsing in.

David took another sip of his coffee, and then a larger gulp. "I'll pick you up at six-thirty. Or do you need more time? When does the market end?"

"Four, but I'll be home by five. It's plenty of time." I could always unpack the next morning if I felt I needed more time.

He took a final sip and set his coffee down. "Thanks for the coffee."

Libby smiled, more like beamed. "Anytime, David."

I walked him to the landing. "Thank you for the flowers."

"Of course. They are almost as pretty as you." With that, he leaned forward and placed a delicate kiss upon my heated cheek. It was the closest I'd been to sex in seven years. "See you Saturday."

The screen door closed, and I released my breath. "Wow."

"Wow is right." Libby was as lit up as a Christmas tree. "That boy has it bad. And you said he wasn't interested?"

"He sure didn't act like it on Sunday."

"Oh my god, he's smitten. Like totally. Someone's been reading the rule book on being a perfect gentleman. Talk about courting. Wow." She danced back into the kitchen and grabbed our still-full coffees. "And I like that about him. That's a points win in my books. Probably Fran's too, and most definitely Adam's."

"Do you think Adam has anything to do with this?"

He had already spent time in jail for pounding the tar out of a guy that attempted to assault his girlfriend, so I wouldn't put it past him to beg a guy to be interested in me.

She bobbed her head, jumped up, and sat on the counter, something I'd never let my daughter do. "Nah. That's more Mia's style."

Well, my sister better not have had a hand in it. It would be nice to think a guy was interested in me because of *me* and not some weird influence from my family.

"So, what are you going to wear?"

"I have no idea. What's going on around here Saturday night?"

She pulled out her phone and scrolled. "Not much. There's a festival in Moon Bay, but it looks like it's a VIP thing."

"Yeah, that wouldn't be a business fancy." Still, my mind was reeling.

What was I going to wear? And most importantly, what should I wear underneath it all? It needed to be something sexy for sure. Just in case.

Chapter Twelve

Saturday night arrived with as much excitement as Christmas morning. For the first time since I started working in the markets, I actually couldn't wait to be finished and head home. Libby sensed the energy too since she commented I was bouncing more than she usually did.

Racing home, I didn't even unpack the truck. I left it parked beside the garage, praying it didn't rain overnight. After sitting with Vera and listening to her fun-filled adventurous day with Francesca, I placed a kiss on her forehead and went into full date preparation mode. I scrubbed, I shaved, and I lotioned up my arms and legs, making sure I was as sweetly smelling as I was smooth. For some reason, even my hair cooperated as I twisted the sides into loose braids and pinned them at the back in a messy bun. It was soft and romantic looking, and if I did say so myself, it was on point.

Adam arrived promptly at six-fifteen as I didn't want him

there when David arrived. My goal was to get Vera off for the evening and to finish getting dressed. At least hair and makeup were done.

"I hope you're changing?" Adam ran a disapproving gaze over me.

"What? You don't think the sweats are appropriate?" I spun around and ended with a plie.

"Nope." He grabbed Vera's overnight bag and signed for her to bring her favourite stuffy.

"Well, I have a new dress. I'd put it on, but I still have time." Not a lot, but that was the last step. Five minutes tops, or even less if I skipped squeezing into the spanx.

I walked hand in hand with Vera out to Adam's truck. "What will you two be up to this evening?"

Vera signed as she talked. "Star Wars movies."

"All of them?" I raised a brow as I stared at Adam.

He shook his head to me, but I didn't miss the slight nod he sent in Vera's direction. "Of course not. She'll be tucked into bed by nine."

"Hmmm…"

Vera was good with staying up late, however, she was the devil incarnate the next day, even though she typically went to bed early the next night with little fuss.

"Not too late." I wagged my finger. "Nine o'clock at the latest."

"And no junk food." Adam rolled his eyes, but I knew better. Naturally, he would have some of her favourites; part of what made the sleepover a lot of fun. "But I think Summer is bringing something healthier. A muffin or bread or something vegan?" He rubbed his chin. "I forget, but it's homemade and delicious, and works for Vera's delicate system."

"Alright. Well, you two have fun. I'll meet you for brunch."

"Ten-thirty, right? And bring your date." Adam opened the door of his truck, and Vera climbed in. "Put your seatbelt on."

I laughed, watching as Vera did as she was told. "Yeah, I don't think so. A little too soon to introduce him to everyone."

"Fran's met him, Mia has hung out at the restaurant on occasion, and I'm about to meet him. It would just be Mom and Dad who are new."

"And Harrison." My youngest brother hadn't been to a monthly brunch in a few months.

"Yeah, well, he's too busy flaking out on everyone. Mom and Dad are tame."

I shook my head. "I'm not bringing David. We're not even a couple."

"Right." He grinned and bobbed his head. "Francesca gave me all the details. If he isn't now, I highly suspect he will be after tonight."

A little Mini Cooper rounded the corner. Shit, David was early.

"Don't you have a movie marathon to get started?" I started shoving Adam toward his side of the truck.

He glanced down the road, and a brotherly smirk filled his face. "Actually, if you don't mind, I'd like to stay for a minute."

"Get going." My teeth gritted together. The last thing I wanted was for Adam to make a scene.

David pulled in front of the house, leaving room for Adam to back out of the driveway, and stepped out of the car looking as dapper as ever. A step up from his dress pants and button up, David had added a form-fitting suit jacket, ratcheting the hot factor by ten. Damn, did he ever look not put together?

"Hello." I barely breathed out.

He produced two roses from behind his back and handed the red one to me without breaking eye contact. "For you."

"Thank you." I accepted and bowed my head, noticing at that moment how I was still in sweats. Good grief. "I'm changing. In a minute. Just sending Vera and Adam off."

He lifted the other rose. "For Vera. May I?"

I swallowed and blinked. Maybe Libby was right, and he had read some rule book about courting. "She'd like that."

David walked over and handed the pink rose to my daughter. The giant smile on her face was bright enough to glow like a lighthouse beacon. David signed *for a princess,* and she eagerly accepted the flower, stuffing her nose deep into the velvety petals.

I waved and blew a kiss at my daughter as my hands signed.

"Have fun tonight."

David stepped away from the truck as Adam walked closer and shook his hand. "Good to see you again."

"You as well."

Adam turned in my direction. "I can keep David company if you want to get changed."

I grimaced, although my options were clearly limited. There was no way Adam was leaving just yet, and I needed to put a proper outfit on. "Fine. Five minutes. I'll be quick."

My gaze flittered between my date and my brother, who had the unmistakable look of puffing out his chest and making himself taller. Oh shit.

"Be nice." It was a warning for Adam only and judging from the *who me?* look on his face, he knew it too.

I dashed inside, and once behind closed doors was pulling off my t-shirt and dancing my way out of my sweats before I'd even hit my bedroom. In a breath, I kicked everything into the bottom of my closet and removed the navy blue fit and flare dress from the hanger. I'd managed to find the perfect dress at Redux – the secondhand shop in Stewart Surf. Amazingly enough, it seemed to melt off a few pounds, skipping the need for the spanx, which was good as I was wearing some new lacy underthings.

Zipped up and double-checked, I was back at the front door with my purse and keys within the five minutes I'd promised. I stole a quick peek out the door. Adam was still there, his shoulders more relaxed, but David's were the opposite, and the tension on his face was readable. What the hell had Adam said?

Locking up, I closed the door and sauntered out to the guys, giving a *what-do-you-think* look to my daughter.

She signed *wow* and beamed. A little happy bubble formed inside me, knowing, on occasion, I could dress up as more than just a mother.

Adam whistled. "You clean up nicely."

"No," David started, "she's breathtaking."

My cheeks seared, although it was so nice to hear a compliment. "Stop." I walked over to the truck and gave another kiss to Vera, signing a special message to her. "Be a good girl, and I'll see you tomorrow."

David extended the crook of his arm to me. "Shall we?"

"Yes." I turned my head to glance over my shoulder at Adam, a giant smile upon my face. "Take good care of my baby."

"With my life."

David walked me to his car, and like the perfect gentleman he was, opened the door.

I slipped inside and within a few heartbeats, I was waving at my family as we drove away. "I do hope Adam was being friendly?"

"You're a pretty close family, aren't you?"

"Overly protective." I huffed as I readjusted in my seat.

"Yeah, I gathered that." He pointed to the radio, avoiding all eye contact. "Would you like to listen to anything? More Queen? Or maybe some CCR?"

I shook my head. "If it's okay, today, I'd rather enjoy the silence, which is weird, right? Considering my daughter is losing her hearing."

"Why is that weird?"

"I keep trying to have her listen and hear everything, hoping that someday, when her world is silent, she'll be able to remember certain songs and melodies, but sometimes, I personally crave the silence. All the racket can be overwhelming."

"Probably is for her too."

"Oh." I hadn't thought about it that way. I'd been so busy making sure she was exposed to all music and voices and sounds, I'd never considered for a micro-second it was maybe too much.

"But don't beat yourself up. You're doing the best you can, and Vera seems happy and is quite well-behaved."

I nodded, although I wasn't sure. Maybe all mothers worried they weren't doing as well as they could be, or that there was something more they should be doing. I couldn't be the only one, right? Mother's Guilt was a real and identifiable disorder.

But tonight, I was going to try to not be a mother and focus on being a woman. On a date. With a hot older guy.

"So where are we off to tonight?"

Cheshire Bay had one main road which led out onto the highway, and that branched in two directions. The left route turned toward Stewart Surf, and the right would eventually take you to

Courtenay, but there were many turnoffs along either direction, each with a myriad of possibilities.

"A little cove on the edge of the bay. There's a music festival going on, and it sounded amazing and a perfect date activity."

"A music festival, eh? What kind of music?"

David pulled his eyes off the road for just a moment to look at me with a shrug. "Something like jazz?"

"What? You didn't check it out?" How unlike him.

"The band playing is called The Parade, sounded harmless enough." He shrugged.

"What if it's death metal?" It wasn't my jam, but I knew of some who loved it.

"Then I'm sorry in advance." A gentle chuckle filled the air, striking my heart with the low notes. "But we'll be going elsewhere."

"Not a fan?"

He shook his head and his lips curled in disgust. "Makes me want to blow my brains out."

"Tell me how you really feel." I giggled and took in the surroundings as we drove.

The area on either side of the road was rich in greens and browns; the dark hues were my favourite colours. Something about the deeper shades were soothing.

"Personally, I'm hoping it's more relaxing. Had an absolutely insane day today, and I could use a nice, enjoyable evening."

"So, all topics revolving around work are off the table?" I

raised a questioning brow.

"Yes, most respectfully."

"I'm totally on board with that. What about politics and religion?"

His hands briefly slipped from the 10 and 2 positions as he signaled and pulled out onto the highway leading north. "Please, let's not. Can we stick to more pleasant, less controversial topics?"

"Like blueberry pies?"

"Yes."

"And? Did you enjoy yours?"

"Very much. I finished it off within a couple of days." He patted his flat tummy. "Put on a few pounds too."

"You ate the whole pie?"

"Yeah, it was so good, but don't judge me please."

"Too late. Already have." I snickered but tipped my chin down when he didn't look amused.

"What?"

"You don't like death metal, and you're a micromanager. Trust me, the judging has begun." However, I said it playfully, hoping he wouldn't think I was a total bitch for saying it.

"Oh really?" He cocked his brow and let one hand fall from the steering wheel. "What else have you judged?"

My cheeks heated. Leave it to me and my big mouth to say more than I actually had intended.

"Fine." I inhaled and released my breath in one fell swoop,

tossing my hands up in defeat as I picked my words carefully and laced them with sweetness. "Aside from the way you meet with your guests and thank them for their business, the way you get to my daughter's level and talk in her language…" Which warmed my heart like nothing else, "I've also judged your model-worthy looks and your tailored outfits. Sue me."

"And?" There was an undeniable charm hanging off that word.

"And… Well, I think you are a solid guy; the whole package. Totally good-looking, and quite the gentleman."

"Totally good-looking," he repeated. "Why, thank you."

I clutched my hands together. "I'm nothing if not honest."

"Do you want to know if I have judged you?"

I shook my head and focused out the windshield at the long, windy road ahead. "I don't need you to confirm, I know you have. And I get it. There's a not-so-nice title that comes along with the words *single mother*. Trust me, I've heard them all. Small town, right? Everyone forms and vocalizes their opinion and for a while, it's all anyone and everyone will discuss, but only until something new and exciting rolls in. Thankfully, my story wasn't out for long. There's always a bigger fish."

"What *is* your story? You never mention anyone else." His gaze quickly jumped to my naked hand, before returning to the road.

"I come from a big family, two parents, four siblings. We all grew up in the area. I got pregnant with Vera and became a single mother. Started my own company, and well, here I am."

"There's more to you than that."

"Nope."

"No best friends?"

A weak smile surfaced, and I tore my gaze from the road and threw it to him. "Well, I'm not twelve, so I don't actually classify anyone as my best friend. That just sounds like a lot of pressure to put on a person, but yes, I have some dear friends. You've met Libby and Francesca."

"I stand corrected, and you know what, I take it back. The term best friends does have a childish sound to it." He returned his focus to the road, gripping the wheel a little tighter.

"I have more friends though… There's Mia. Plus, on occasion, I hang out with Summer, but mostly because she's dating my brother, oh, and Chloe too."

"Ah, yes, Dr. Tarkin." The way he said her name, there was something there, but I couldn't put my finger on what it was. Hostility? Indifference? It was hard to tell.

"However, that's about it in the friends department. My group isn't large but they're everything to me. So that's about it for me."

"Hmm…" His eyes narrowed for a fraction of a second. "I'm not buying it. There's more to you than that, however, I'm interested in learning all about you, like your likes and dislikes. Do you like desserts?"

"Who doesn't?"

He looked deep into my eyes. "My ex. She was afraid even the tiniest piece of chocolate cake would make her fat, so she never touched the stuff."

"Wow. I just avoid it when I'm out because it's pricey, and I can typically make it at home for much cheaper."

"Have you always been frugal?"

I recoiled. "You say it like it's a bad word."

"Oh gosh, I'm sorry if that's how it sounds. It wasn't meant to. I just mean, have you always lived paycheque to paycheque?"

Obviously, it had been easy to see how he got to that assumption. My accommodation was average, and the furniture was second-hand.

"Yup. I have a slight petty cash fund for emergencies, but I don't use it. Every activity is well planned out, however, I don't want Vera to lack much."

"You're doing a great job."

"Thank you. You really dazzled her with the rose and the ASL. She'll remember that for a long time."

The speedometer climbed slightly above the speed limit.

"Does her father see her often?"

I snorted and rolled my hands into tight fists as I watched the rush of trees zoom by. "He's no longer allowed, and it's going to stay that way."

The last time I saw Quinn was at the courthouse in Victoria when Vera was still a newborn, and he'd signed over all his parental rights. As part of the hush deal, his family had also deposited a large sum into my bank account, for the express purpose of putting a down payment on a house, which I finally found a couple of years later. When Quinn and his family walked away, I flipped them all the bird. That was the last I'd ever seen of the Stephens family.

"Sorry for bringing it up."

"Sorry, I didn't mean to be snappy, you didn't know. The father figures in her life are my father, Adam, Mia's boyfriend Zachary, and Harrison, whenever he decides to show up." The joys of being a young adult with zero responsibilities.

"That's your little brother?"

"Yeah. Harrison's a tour guide with a whale-watching company up in Stewart, but mainly Adam is the real male fixture in her life, and I love their relationship."

"Family is important."

"To me, it's everything."

"Well…" He tipped his head from side to side. "Not everything."

"You're not close to your family?"

He snorted. "Not anymore. It was just me and my mom for a number of years."

"Oh, I'm sorry. No father?" I took a chance when I asked, and nearly recoiled at his answer.

"The asshole left Mom and me behind in exchange for another. I haven't seen him since I was twelve." A low growl briefly rolled out. "I have zero use for people like that."

There was a rawness to the edge of his words, the kind that had me wanting to dig and not shy away from. Clearly, there was more to his story than he was letting on.

What was he hiding? Did he have secrets like me?

Chapter Thirteen

We turned toward Moon Bay and drove along the edge of the sea, glittering like orange diamonds in the evening sun. Sinking deeper into the seat, I kept my gaze on the tuffs of tall reeds lining the road.

Without further conversation, we pulled into a makeshift parking lot under a giant banner decorated with music notes and the words Mount Wizard Music Festival.

David stopped at the gate and produced two tickets to the guard, who waved us over onto a patch of grass to park. He grabbed a blanket from the trunk and extended an elbow in my direction, which I happily took.

Walking beyond the grassy area, past the myriad of food truck options which were making my mouth water and stomach growl with their enchanting aromas, we headed to the top of the hill overlooking the stage nestled deep in the valley.

He immediately shook open the blanket and smoothed it out. "Figured, if we set up here, we can hear the music, but yet still have a conversation."

I had to agree. If we were lower into the bowl, it would be way louder. Plus, we were off to the side so not in a high-traffic area, and if we turned our heads to the left, we could watch the sailboats float on by.

"I like this, it's truly perfect."

"Have a seat, and I'll grab us some drinks. Anything you don't like?"

I shook my head. "Nah, I'm pretty receptive to anything cold."

He gave his bearded chin a thoughtful rub. "Something cold coming right up."

I stretched out my legs in front of me, crossing them at the ankles, thankful I hadn't worn the spanx; I would've been cut in half trying to sit in them for an extended period of time. My flats hung from the tips of my toes so I flipped them off and watched them fall to the wayside and then allowed my gaze to roam the sights.

Having never been to a music festival, this was a brand-new experience. So many people, just like the markets, and I was sure, had Summer known, she could've collaborated with them and set up a pop-up market or something. I needed to remember to tell her about this the next time I saw her. Would be great for her business and the vendors.

"For you."

I jumped as he handed me an amber-coloured plastic cup. There was a smidge of condensation on the cup, and it slipped a little as I grabbed it.

"Thanks."

"It's a pear-based ale. I forget what they called it."

I removed the lid and took a sip. Definitely had a subtle pear aftertaste, but overall, was quite delicious. "Wow."

"Right? I should look into getting this for the restaurant." He sat beside me, stretching out, and leaning on his right side.

"Do you have many on tap beers?"

"Only a few." He listed them off, not that I knew any of them, however, I was sure Francesca would, having worked in the bar. "But with the renovations, I could always add another one or two."

"You could."

He took a sip of his beer and lowered his head. "I told myself I wasn't going to ask…"

I started laughing, somehow knowing exactly what was on his mind. "The mural is coming along just fine. You can take a peek when you drop me off, although there isn't much to see yet, but I can show you what the plans are."

"I'd like that." He connected with me.

"But for the rest of the night, no talk of work, okay?"

He raised his plastic cup, ready to knock it against mine. "Deal."

"Good." After a clink, I let the beer linger on my tastebuds. I needed a few of these to hang out in the shop – a reward for completing a piece or something.

Remembering our earlier conversation about music tastes, I spoke. "So, we should come up with a Plan B, in case this turns out to be death metal or something."

"Well, if we judge the music based on what the crowds are typically wearing, I think we're safe."

I gazed around. Women milled about in long, flowy skirts or soft, comfortable-looking clothes, and the men dressed in a wild assortment from completely casual in shorts and tank tops to nice dress pants and shirts, like David. There were a definite lack of dark, goth-like clothing or people wearing chains and dog collars. Yeah, this crowd didn't scream death metal.

"I think you're right."

"However," he sat up, "having a backup plan isn't a bad idea."

"Especially with those clouds building, although there's not supposed to be a storm."

"Nope. Weather forecast looks good, in that regard. Maybe some rain overnight."

"Ooh, I like the rain." I took another drink. "Especially walking Main Street at night, just after the fact. It's like the streets are shiny, and it has this enchanting appeal, like something out of a tv show. One of my favourite things to do, but I don't get out much to do it."

"What do you like to do for fun?" David gave me his full attention.

"Well, Vera is my life so when we're together, we love to watch movies and go to the park. There's a new park near downtown."

"But as an adult?"

"Well, aside from the rain walks when Fran can watch Vera, because Vera hates getting wet, I don't go out much. She doesn't even like splashing in the ocean." Or at all.

"Really? I find that hard to believe. We're a seaside town." He shook his head. "But as an adult, you don't do much either?"

I shrugged. "I know it's weird, but when I wholeheartedly accepted I was going to be a mom, I dove in headfirst, with zero regrets." After all, it was earth-shattering to learn I was infertile, so to be blessed with pregnancy was a dream come true, even if the circumstances leading up to it weren't ideal. There's nothing I wouldn't do for my daughter.

David was watching me intently, his gaze circling my face, and I realised I needed to say something more, so I wasn't this boring person who did nothing in her minimal spare time.

"I don't have a lot of girlfriends, but on occasion, we'll get together and have a beer at Amber's Ale or something but that's more a rare treat than a normal occurrence."

"And you're okay with that?" He sounded displeased, like

there was more to life than what I was living, which was only partly true. Everybody wished for more than they had, but the reality was, I had to make the best of what I had.

"Corny, right? But I'd rather be with Vera and soak up as much of her childhood as I could get. My parents didn't spend a lot of time with us growing up, and we always had babysitters. Almost weekly, until I became of age to babysit, and then they saved their babysitting fees and put it towards their weekly events. Dad always said Mom was his number one, and he lived to please her. We were an afterthought."

"Sounds like you had it rough."

I shook my head and backtracked. "No, no, no. Oh please, don't think that. I had a great childhood. I'm just saying my parents missed out on so much with me, and my siblings, that I don't want to do that with Vera. For as long as she can, I'll attend every one of her sporting events or musical performances or plays."

"And when she's completely lost her hearing?" His smile turned downward.

Mine ramped up. "They'll still have activities; it'll just be different from what you and I are used to, but you can guarantee I'll still be there."

"That's great. Involved parents are a rarity it seems. Can't tell you how many ignorant folks I see in the dining room, letting their brats run around while their phones hold their attention. It's infuriating and customers get upset, especially with the kids who feel the need to tantrum tables away from those who brought them into the world." He sighed and looked toward the stage in the basin of the hill. "I had to raise my prices slightly to deter some of them."

"Did it work?" How interesting it was that he raised his prices. I had done the same on his project, but I pretty much had the same amount of guilt ribboning through the idea as he did through his words.

"Sadly, yes."

"Why sadly?"

"Because rather than being affordable to the masses, now I cater to a smaller crowd." His voice wasn't as strong as his previous rant.

"But if it's a more pleasant customer experience, shouldn't that outweigh the slight increase?" Sure, I was grasping.

He shrugged. "Maybe. I just don't want to be known as the place that hates kids."

"Did you mention that when you raised your prices?" I cocked a brow.

"No."

"Then I think you're safe." I rubbed his leg, trying not to focus on the strong thigh beneath the soft material of his pants. Jesus, I needed help. "Besides, a couple of negative reviews won't hurt in the long run, right?"

"Yeah, a couple I can handle, but there's this one, or maybe a bunch of copycats all using the same hashtag, who keep trashing the place. I haven't even sold that particular product for the last couple of years."

I swallowed. Since having signed a contract with David, I'd stopped leaving nasty reviews, and as it was, it had been at least a few months, probably longer, since I'd even thought about leaving one. Figured it was over and done with. Perhaps I needed to check the reviews and see if they were originating from one of my accounts, which would be exceptionally weird since even I couldn't remember the passwords.

I tipped back my beer a little more and swallowed down the top quarter. "I wouldn't let it worry you then. If your die-hard customers know that fact, then I think you're good."

"Still, I aim for perfection."

"I think you're nailing it." I hadn't meant for it to slip out, but once it was said it was too late to take it back, not that I would've. David was pretty damn amazing. "No more talk of work though." I winked.

The music started playing, and he had been right. We were in the perfect spot to hear it, but not have it overwhelm any conversation. Which we needed to start up again. The silence was hard, but as I raked my gaze over him, he was taking in the sweet melodies. His eyes were closed, his head tipped back slightly, and a small smile teased at the corner of his perfect pout.

I let him listen without interruption until the song finished, and the band introduced themselves. "Did you know that song?"

"The song yes, but not that band. They must be a cover band or something, but I really liked their version."

"I could tell." I leaned back on my hands, stretching and pointing my toes.

Another song started, and this one with a punchier beat. Some couples in the basin jumped onto their feet and started dancing.

David looked at them, and then at me. "Want to?"

"Want to what?" My gaze widened.

"Dance?"

"Here? There's no dance floor."

"Who cares? It's a music festival. Come on, let's move." He got onto his feet and extended a hand. "Come on. Unless you can't dance?"

I didn't really want to, not with people hanging around us on their picnic blankets, ready to stare and judge, however, his words challenged me, and in a flash, I was on my feet. To hell with what others thought.

We hopped and bopped, and by the third song, a person ten years younger than me took over my body and let the music move through to my soul as the cover band played an old Whitney Houston song. It was so freeing to move my body, and truly dance like no one was watching. If they had been, I didn't notice. I laughed and wiggled around, having more fun in those few minutes than I had in a long time.

The cover band, whose name I didn't catch, played a few fast

147

songs before starting a slower song.

David offered his hand, and when I accepted, he slowly placed it above his shoulders. My hands linked together around his neck as his arms hooked around my waist and we swayed with the melody.

"I don't think I know this song," I whispered, even though we were outside.

"It's about seeing a person's true colours, and I see yours." He was smiling as he stared deeply into my eyes.

"How's that?" I pressed closer, loving the feeling of being held.

"You're beautiful, and you want to be everything to everyone, but sometimes you need to be you to the outside world. I loved watching you dance; you were so unencumbered and free."

I buried my face into his shirt. Damn, he smelled so good.

"Don't be ashamed. It was magical."

"Magical? I've never had my dancing called magical." I wanted to smile, but a heartbeat of shame kept me from making the change.

"Fine, chaotic? Like someone having a spell? Is that better?" He was borderline laughing, and although it was directed at my wild dance moves, there was a warm current running through his tone. He wasn't being mean; he had actually enjoyed watching me dance.

"No, I prefer the magical version."

"I adored it. I adore you." He stared into my eyes. "I've never quite met anyone like you before."

"Really? Never?" There were a few thousand people in this town.

"Really." His gaze danced between my eyes as we both stopped moving, although my heart rate climbed like I'd run a thousand stairs.

My breath caught in the back of my throat, and I stared into the depths of his dark blues.

"I've wanted to kiss you, you know, for quite some time now."

I swallowed, my gaze following the movement of his lips. "You did?"

"Ever since you baked with me. But I wasn't sure how to find the right moment."

"This could be one."

"It is." And as if in slow motion, he inched closer, slowly, teasingly, almost with a borderline hesitation.

I pushed through the rest of the tiny distance and pressed my wanton lips onto his.

It was everything a kiss should be – delicate and soft, and warm and breathy.

He pulled back and looked down at me. "That was…"

My heart stopped beating for a fraction of a second as I waited for him to finish speaking.

"Amazing. I should've done it a long time ago." Suddenly, a

twinkle appeared in his eyes, lighting him up in a way it took years off him. "I like kissing you."

"I like kissing you."

It was then I knew I was in big, big trouble.

Chapter Fourteen

We kissed some more, until a couple walked by with plates of steamy food and tantalizing scents.

"That looked really good," he said, as he followed them all the way to their spot. "Hungry?"

I slowly nodded. I was hungry for another taste of his pear beer-flavoured lips. "Sure, I can eat."

"I don't want to grab something you don't like, since I know you have an aversion to chicken."

How sweet he remembered, even if it wasn't an aversion. It's not that I didn't like chicken, I just preferred mine well cooked, not bright pink and stuffed with salmonella.

Hand in hand, we strolled through food truck row, and of all the food choices, finally selected donairs. It had been years since I had them, and the picture of them on the side of the truck looked too good to pass up.

With our plates, we headed back to our blanket and settled down.

I held the meat-filled pita with two hands, and as I took a bite, David raised his brow. Seeing it from his point of view, it probably looked quite erotic, and since the beer was hitting me nicely, I was going to play it up. I opened my mouth wide and put my lips over the top, biting down slowly, all the while looking deep into his eyes.

His Adam's apple bobbed, and he gave his lips a quick lick.

If I wasn't mistaken, there was a little splash of colour tinting his cheeks beneath his whiskers.

"Are you enjoying that?"

I swallowed down the bite, and reached for a napkin, dabbing at the corners of my mouth. "Very much so. You?"

"Oh, I'm enjoying this, yes."

I continued to slowly tease and taunt him with my seductive donair eating, but I hoped it wasn't all for nothing. If David wanted me, even to get to first base, I was not going to stop him. I wanted him and hoped my playfulness was a subtle enough cue.

He chowed down on his food, somehow not spilling a drop of sauce anywhere, whereas I had to keep wiping at my mouth.

"Missed a spot." He took his napkin and brushed it over my cheek.

The skin tingled beneath his touch, and I couldn't help myself – my breath caught again in my throat.

"Do you want to get out of here?"

152

"And go where?" My voice was breathless, and I chided myself for being so easy.

"There's this great pier down the street from my house. With a bitching view of the sunset."

It wasn't quite what I had in mind, nonetheless, I agreed.

After we parked at his garage, we sauntered hand-in-hand down the road toward the ocean. The street was deserted, as was the boardwalk extending out to the ocean. Our shoes clacked against the wooden beams, and in wanting to preserve the peace and quiet, I bent down and removed my shoes.

"Do you like being barefoot?"

"Yeah. Even in winter. Don't you?"

He shook his head and gave my hand a little squeeze. "I'm not a foot person. I always keep mine covered with socks."

"Even when you're sleeping?" I laughed.

"Well, no. I tend to sleep naked."

My heart hammered in my chest, and I tucked a strand of hair behind my ear, trying to feign off an incoming rush of heat to my cheeks. "I can't sleep naked."

"Probably not a good idea with little ones around."

"No." My voice lowered, and all I could imagine was his tight body on full display. In my mind, I peeked under the covers; it was perfection.

"Check it out." He nudged to the horizon.

I've seen some damn amazing sunsets in my life, having lived beside the ocean forever, but that one? It blew them all away. The edge of the water was lined in ambers and mandarins, slowly fading upwards into corals and lavender overhead. The sky to the east was darker shades of indigo and violets, and it was enough to take my breath away, along with my voice.

David wrapped his arms around me, his chin above my shoulder, his lips beside my ear. "It's almost as beautiful as you."

I turned to him, gazing into his eyes, and stretched up onto the tips of my toes. With his face between my palms, I tipped my head slowly and brushed my lips across his, unleashing a powerful response.

He lifted me, and I wrapped my legs around him. As he walked, my butt bumped into the railing, and he set me on top. I couldn't stop kissing him, and I parted my lips to give him full rights to explore. Naturally, he did not disappoint, and the heat from his tongue moving in sync with mine radiated out to the tips of my fingers but stopped momentarily to stoke my embers. I was on fire.

His kisses trailed south, along my neck, and his body pushed harder against mine.

"Not here," I whispered. "Please."

He pulled back and stared into my eyes. "No problem." With a tip of his head in the direction of his house. "My place or yours?"

I didn't want to wait any longer than was needed and kill the mood. "Yours works."

He kissed me again and helped me off the railing.

We practically race-walked back, and by the time he opened the door, my body was humming with anticipation, but now that we were here, and ready to go, a new wave of emotions took over.

I suddenly felt like I was nineteen all over again. Would I know what to do? Would I do it right? Could I make him feel desired?

I needn't have worried, once he placed those firm lips on me, my inhibitions went to the wayside. Once again, he lifted me and walked me to his counter, setting me on the spot where blueberry pies had once sat, the coolness seeping in through my thin dress. His powerful kisses turned me on, his velvety tongue robbed my mind of useless thoughts and worries, and his deft hands caressing my arms heated me from the inside out.

I wrapped my legs tighter around his waist, pressing my soaked panties against him, as my hands explored his strong back muscles beneath my fingertips.

Breathing harder than I had before, I moaned when his hand found my knee, and slowly pushed under my skirt.

Inching tenderly, he touched my thigh, then my hip, and his thumb grazed over my little belly pouch, forcing my breath to lodge deep in my chest. I wanted this. I wanted him. To feel him inside me, to feel once again what it would be like to experience a man-given orgasm, and not one self-produced.

Before my gasp became audible, he gently cupped my panty-covered ass and pulled me tight to his firm body. Once more, our tongues sought each other out and moved together in perfect

155

synchronization.

My body was ready to explode, and he hadn't so much as put a finger in me yet.

"God, you are so beautiful." He cupped my ass cheek, moving down and under, while staring into my soul, bypassing my eyes.

"You're quite the man yourself." I could barely breathe as his finger touched the edge of my panties. Right. There. I need to focus, or I'd be done before the fun truly started.

My gaze lowered to the buttons on his shirt, and daring myself, I started undoing them, one at a time, inhaling slowly with each push through the hole. I pulled his soft shirt free of his pants, kissing his incredible collarbone. My heart beat so hard I was sure it was visible.

"You're sure you want to do this?" He tipped my chin up.

"Yes."

With that confirmation, he bent down and kissed me again, breathing a new life into where one hadn't been before.

I pushed the shirt up and over his shoulders, the muscly strength beneath the tips of my fingertips. My dreams hadn't lied – he was perfection. Totally and truly.

Removing his hand from beneath my skirt, as my heart plummeted, he moved it to the back of my dress, kissing and searching for the release.

"It's a zipper, on the side." I moved my hand there and

fingered the little pull, sliding it downward.

Effortlessly he set me back onto the floor where I slowly pulled my arms free of the dress and felt it flutter past my legs as it puddled at my feet. Instinctively, I covered my chest.

"Don't," he whispered as his face closed in on mine and his heated breath tickled my ears. "You're too beautiful to be covered up."

His hands seemed larger than life as he wrapped them around my waist and gripped my nearly naked ass. A soft moan escaped his lips, but it could've been mine. My skin felt alive, and every touch, every caress, was intensified a thousand percent. It was the greatest feeling.

My hands fumbled with his belt buckle, my lack of experience showing through, but I managed to release them, and he stepped out, kicking them off to the side. Clad only in our underwear, he lifted me back up to his waist and carried me through his kitchen, and into the bedroom tucked behind. As if I were fine china, and I'd break in a heartbeat, he set me down on his soft, silky bed.

"You're stunning." His gaze raked from the tip of my head to my feet and seductively returned to settle on my core.

It was likely shooting flames if the throbbing sensation was any indication.

Like a panther, he inched toward me and dropped to his knees. The whiskers from his cheeks as he kissed up the inside of my thighs drove me crazy. Like a thousand little tingles all happening at once. He nuzzled his nose in between the center of my legs, which I had slowly parted to welcome him in.

Keeping my eyes closed, I concentrated on the heat, on the throbbing, on the wet kisses atop my panties. I wanted them off, to give him full access, but didn't want to be greedy. He kissed through the silk and slowly a finger ran along the seam, slipping under and pulling them off to the side.

Sweet baby Jesus.

His tongue lapped as he dipped a finger into me, and I nearly shuddered from the experience. Slowly, he probed, and tickled, and pressed his sweet lips against me, licking and tasting and finding the spot that made me growl when he pressed his flat tongue against it and rubbed. My hands gripped the sheets, and I arched my back, forcing his face to bury deeper into my pleasure.

As he deepened his exploration with his fingers, his tongue teased against me, and I was unable to control myself. I fought it as long as I could, but a quick flick, followed by a tiny suck at the same time as he fingered me deep, was my greatest undoing. Although my eyes were closed, I saw stars and colours, and a voice I didn't recognize growled out of me, filling the room with its gratified sound.

"Oh, David." My breath came in waves. "Oh my god."

He covered my mouth in kisses, and for the first time in my whole life, I tasted myself; all sweet and savoury. A bit of a turn-on, not that I needed any more help.

He reached over me and into the drawer beside the bed, fumbling for a condom. Expertly, he rolled it over his length and lay prone on his back.

A night full of firsts, since I'd never been on top before, but I couldn't wait to try. Feeling wildly alive and unabashedly free, I straddled him, and it gave him full access to my bouncing breasts, which he stared at. As I maneuvered over him, he guided his thickness into the right spot, having first tested it with his fingers. I was still on fire. Slowly, I lowered over him, feeling him fill me up in the best way.

"Lean back and use my thighs for support." His own words were breathless.

Unsure, I did as he suggested. While his one hand palmed my breast, with the thumb focused on my erect nipple, his other hand slipped back between my legs and searched out my pleasure zone.

I rolled forward in ecstasy, but found it wasn't quite as stimulating when I cut off access, so trying to remind myself to keep breathing, I leaned back. This time, both his hands moved to squeeze my hips and he rocked me back and forth over his pelvis, until his thumbs slipped a little lower and worked me back into a frenzy.

As I bucked my hips with all the sensations rocketing through my body, he pumped his pelvis and his thumbs rubbed and circled and pressed. The harder I moved, the firmer the pressure, and I was sure I would explode all over him once more. When he released the pressure and instead made teasing little touches, I squeezed his thighs as another orgasmic wave crashed over me and threatened to wash me out. With that, he grabbed my hips and moved me back and forth, the speed increasing the longer he held his breath, until finally, he grunted and groaned, his hands dropped to the sides in satisfaction.

Fighting to catch his breath, he blew the words out. "Damn, Erin, that was magnificent."

"I agree."

My pounding heartbeat made my words as erratic as my thoughts, and I did the only thing to come to mind, and that was lay beside him, pressing my back against his firm wall of a chest.

Laying in his arms, sweaty and spent, I couldn't wait to do it again. It had been far too long since sex made me feel this good, this lit up inside, like I could take on the world.

Chapter Fifteen

Waking up in the morning, snuggled under David's heavy arm was a new one. Yet it felt perfectly natural.

"Good morning," he said, as he kissed my bare shoulder.

I rolled over and stared into his handsome face. "Good morning."

"That was some night, last night."

"Best I ever had." My heart was as full as my body was exhausted. It was a tremendous feeling.

"Really?"

"Why do you sound so surprised?" I pressed my naked body against him.

"Because you're you, and gorgeous. Every man's dream." He lazily ran a fingertip over my hips. When he did that at three am, it led to another round of the best sex ever, for the third time.

"And what about you? You were married, surely you had

many nights like that?"

His gaze flipped to the ceiling. "Never. She was a one-and-done type, typically heading straight to the shower afterward. There was no cuddling, and I wasn't allowed to sleep with my arm around her."

"Guess that's why you divorced her, huh." The words slipped out before I could stop them.

"Well, that was part of it. Where she wouldn't do that with me, she had no problems snuggling with someone else."

"Oh, Jesus, I'm sorry." All my life I'd never understood why people cheat. Just man up and end things first, how hard was that?

After pulling the sheet over my naked body, I rested my head on his shoulder and trailed my fingers around his tight chest.

"It is what it is. She moved on, but it was the darkest point in my life." His voice softened, but his body tensed. "About seven years ago, I discovered the truth. In my own house, no less. I kicked her out, dumped all her things on the lawn, and sold the place."

"Was that here in Cheshire Bay?"

"No. I commuted in from Stewart Surf."

A bit of a drive, but not ridiculous.

"Then I bought this place. But I was angry. So angry. At everything and everybody. My lawyer screwed me over, and I ended up having to cut the ex a cheque, until I found out, via another lawyer, who was amazing, how the ex was actually screwing around on me." He spit out the words, and he tensed harder beneath my body.

162

My head rose and fell with his quick breaths.

"However, her parents were a different matter, as they were investors, and I needed to buy them out as the divorce proceedings went through." He sighed, and I tightened my grip around him.

"To make matters worse, I went into heavy debt and was a wreck. A train wreck really. I yelled at everyone; employees included. My turnover, at that point, was sky-high. In three months, I think I went through fifteen staff, which maybe doesn't sound like much—"

"But considering the town…"

"Yeah. Good help is hard enough to find, but when the boss is a dick? No one wanted to work for me, and I was stretched as thin as could be. Complaints came in left and right, and I dismissed every single one of them."

"And when was that again?"

He faced me and without skipping a beat, had his answer ready. "First quarter of the year, seven years ago."

I did the quick math in my head. That's when I was pregnant with Vera. That's when I got food poisoning from undercooked chicken, and nearly lost my baby. That's why when I called to complain and demanded restitution, he shot me down. Not only was I at the end of my rope, but he had also nearly wrapped his own around his neck.

Suddenly, I felt like shit.

I kissed his shoulder and held him tight. "I'm sorry your wife and her family put you through the wringer."

"I'm better now. I've had time to heal and make amends. That's all I can do, right?"

I swallowed. "I guess."

"Now you go." He twisted onto his side and searched my face for the passage into my soul.

"Say again?"

"That's how this works. I open up to you and share something dark about my past, and in return, you do the same thing."

My internal gates slammed shut. "I don't have anything dark in my past." At least nothing I'd ever give voice to. He didn't need to know all my secrets, it was traumatizing recalling them as it was, and this moment didn't call for a flash flood of raw, painful emotions.

"No, nothing at all?"

I shrugged, playing innocent. "I hate to admit it, but I'm pretty damn boring."

"You most definitely are not. Last night was…"

His kiss robbed me of rational thoughts, as his deft tongue and lips aroused me, building a deep throbbing sensation between my legs.

His palms slipped under the sheet but over my hips. "What do you say we have a little fun, and then I whip you up a breakfast."

"As much as I want to, I can't." A grimace leaked out of my soul and onto my face. I so wanted another round of feeling him move inside me, or that deep connection, that moment of losing yourself to the experience. "I'm meeting my family for brunch. In an hour. I really should get home and changed."

"I'll take you home, on one condition."

"What's that?"

He kissed me quickly. "Can I see you again tonight?"

"Like after Vera's in bed?

"Not quite what I was thinking." A lazy smile appeared. "But if that works, sure?"

"You want me to sneak you in?"

He roiled, putting some distance between us. "I hate that word."

I mentally face-palmed. Of course, he did. One of the reasons he left his wife. Or she left him.

"I can knock gently on the back door after nine-thirty. She's asleep by then, right?"

"Most of the time."

The sweetest expression, the kind that was borderline puggy-doggish with a cute little pout built on his perfect face. "So? It's not like she'd hear us."

And as much as I didn't like that phrase, there was truth to it. "I still can't. I'm not sure yet how to tell Vera about us."

I twisted away as the words hung between us because I wasn't sure what we were. Boyfriend-girlfriend? Friend with benefits? I really didn't know. This was all new territory to me.

* * *

Fran, Vera, and I came back home from brunch, and as I pulled into the driveway, I spotted a big bouquet of flowers sitting on the front porch.

Vera signed *who from?* and let out a little squeal.

Fran sighed. "Well, isn't he just the cutest?"

I shrugged and answered Vera. "I don't know."

"D-A-V-I-D." Fran's fingers spelled out his name for Vera's benefit.

"Let's see." I parked the car, but Vera beat me to the flowers, handing me the card.

Fran waltzed over and read the card over my shoulder.

> *To Erin,*
> *Thanks for your patience and for the*
> *wonderful date. A surprise is coming*
> *your way, watch for it.*
> *D.*

Wow. The guy was a total dream.

"Well, we didn't get all the details on the date." Fran wiggled her brows and grabbed the door while I ushered in the bouquet. "But it looks like it was a huge success."

The amazing scent from the colourful flowers warmed my insides, not quite the way David had last night, several times over, but still.

I set them on the table, next to the red rose from last night.

Vera giggled and signed *l o v e.*

"No, it's not love. It's too early for that, so don't be getting any ideas in your head." I turned to Francesca. "And stop putting those ideas there."

"Who me?" She had the audacity to look surprised, but I knew her better than she thought. Still, her smile never faded, and neither did mine.

"I really should get out in the workshop and keep at his mural."

My sister was practically dancing around the kitchen, stopping every few seconds to smell the flowers.

"Would you stop?" I asked.

"But it's sooo sweet." Her perma-grin was larger than life.

I sighed, after inhaling the floral scent myself. "What are you up to for the afternoon?"

"I'm going to finish painting downstairs and start putting together the paperwork. With school having already started, I want to make sure I have everything ready to go. I plan on hanging up signs in the main entrance."

"Post in the Bugle as well."

"Yeah, but that costs money. Personal interaction I can do for free."

She had a point.

"I have a free website to set up, and I'm posting some pictures. I've been trying to connect a social media account to it all, but I've been struggling. So, I'm meeting with Lily this afternoon. She's a tech genius apparently."

"Genius – code for very expensive."

"She's not ridiculous, but she said she'd do it for a swap. Ten free drop-ins for her son Henry while she runs to her midwife appointments and attends to some errand running."

Fran was a smart girl, and I was immediately proud of her for swapping services. It's exactly what I would've done as well. "Let me know how things go with Lily. I may look into swapping with her too."

"Oh, you going to rework your website?"

"Sure. Yeah, of course." It could use a refreshing, or attention for that matter.

An idea suddenly brewed. Maybe she could help me wipe out all my comments and negative reviews on Birch Bay Burgers. There were a lot, and I couldn't remember all the places I left them, but if she was a tech genius, she'd be able to find them and wipe them all away, right?

"I'm heading to my room for a nap." Francesca hung off the door frame in the kitchen. "Like you, I had a late night too."

"What? With who?"

"Jeremy."

I shook my head. He was new.

"I'm seeing him again tonight too." She walked a few steps. "Wake me by three, if I'm not back up."

"Hey, Vera," I called out her name, signing, "Want to come and play with the wood?"

She shook her head and let her hands do the talking. *Video games?*

"Didn't you play enough last night with Uncle Adam?"

"Star Wars." She spoke slowly and then yawned.

Although he said they only watched the first one, I wouldn't be surprised if they'd watched at least part of the second one too. That would've put her way over her usual bedtime. But that may have also worked to my advantage. If she stayed up too late, she'd likely crash early. If she crashed early, I could properly thank a certain Mr. Good in Bed. And with Fran going out tonight, it was too perfect.

"For now, you can play one hour of video games." She'd grabbed her iPad before I'd even grabbed my phone from the depths of my pocket. "I need to make a call first."

I dialed David's number, and he answered on the second ring.

"I have an embarrassingly large bouquet of flowers in my house. Thank you so much."

"Ah, good. You got them. I didn't want to show up again unannounced."

"It's all good. Thank you." I gazed upon them with growing love. David really was the sweetest. "Why don't you come over tonight? You can see the work I'm doing on your mural."

Please sense the hint in my voice.

"Love to. When?"

I hope he heard it. "Six-thirty?"

Yes, Vera would still be awake, but that was okay. Maybe she could get used to seeing him, then it wouldn't be so bam-in-the-face kind of flip if or when David and I took things to the next level.

"See you then." The line went dead but not before my heart did a little pitter-patter.

Chapter Sixteen

avid arrived right at six-thirty, not a second later, and brought with him a dozen cookies. "For you."

"Cookies." Vera signed with excitement.

I shook my head. "No way. You're tired, and you'll get a sugar rush which won't help you sleep."

She stomped her feet and crossed her arms over her chest, an angry pout curled her bottom lip. If it hadn't been the tenth time today she'd done that exact same look, it may have been cute.

"Maybe tomorrow, after breakfast, before you get on the bus."

The first bus ride to the school. I'd taken her on the first two days last week, but with any luck, moving forward she'd be on the bus which would give me a little more working time.

"No. Now." She took her first two fingers and tapped them hard against her thumb, following it by extending her pinkie and thumb out to the side, tightly closed palm facing her, and yanked her arms down to her hips. Her signing was angry, her wrists were rigid and unyielding. My child was over tired. Big time.

"Absolutely not. And if you keep it up, you won't get one after breakfast either." I put my metaphorical foot down, signing as I spoke, while embarrassment washed over me as Vera made a scene in front of David. Last thing I wanted was to look like a pushover, or on the opposite side of the spectrum as a hard-assed parent.

The stare-down started from her to me, but I cocked my brow and crossed my arms over my chest, leaning in her direction just a bit. When she blinked and backed up, it was over.

"Now, I'm going to show David his artwork, but I'll be back in a few minutes. You can go and play with your Barbies. Stay here." I made a similar gesture, like her *now* sign, except when my pinkie and thumb were extended, my palms faced the floor and I made a tighter movement. "Stay."

Her gaze volleyed between me and David, and whatever battle she was fighting in her head failed to surface, she spun on her feet and stormed off to her bedroom.

I stole a cookie when she was out of earshot. Damn, it was so soft and chewy – and the perfect escape for a heartbeat – I could've wiped out the whole box right there. I offered one to David.

"Let's go out to the shop."

He followed me out, and once we were inside and the door was closed, he spun me around and kissed me, pushing me up against

172

the wall of my shop. I quickly threaded my fingers through his thick hair, and plunged my tongue into his, tasting remnants of the chocolate and sweet cookie crust. Surprisingly, it was so hot, and had Vera not been within close distance, I would've seen how far we could've gone. A fantasy come to life.

Instead, as he was planting kisses on my collarbone and stoking the embers that had failed to cool, I pushed him away.

"After, when she'll be in bed. Plus, my sister's out on a date so we can have a little fun."

The heat between my legs was pulsing. I needed relief, and maybe some help for feeling this way with a guy. Wasn't it unusual to have such strong feelings so early into a relationship? David was so sweet, and so likeable, even if years ago he was a complete jerk to me *one time*. Knowing him now, and hanging out with him, generated these unique emotions of wanting to explore things more. Was that how a grown-up relationship worked?

I'd need to ask Fran or Libby, but I didn't want to let on how generally inexperienced I was in this arena. Relationships weren't my strength. They weren't even in my top thirty list of things I was good at. Besides, my serious last boyfriend had been Vera's father, and that was a relatively short relationship.

"So, show me the pieces."

Catching my breath, I swallowed and led him over to the side of the shop where the booth pieces were stacked. Against the wall, I flipped through the stacks and produced the first five layers.

"All are cut but need to be stained. I'll be doing that on Friday, so they have the weekend to set. Then next week I'll be able to assemble them and give them the finishing touches." I laid them out as I had planned and lifted them to show David. "They'll look like this."

He ran a hand through his hair and blew out. "That's amazing. They're going to look so good in the place. You've done a great job."

"Thank you." A faint heat I hoped wasn't noticeable, seared beneath the apples of my cheeks.

"And the mural?"

I set the pieces back in the right spots, as each layer was being stained a different colour, and walked over to the other corner. "This is proving to be a little more challenging."

"Oh? How come?"

"To be honest, the size of it." I grabbed one length of board, and set it across my workspace. "But, and hear me out, I think I figured out how to make it work. I'll need to carve and detail in smaller sections, but I can dovetail it all together and it should be pretty seamless."

"Should be?" He raised a critical brow, although there was a small twitch of a smile threatening to escape and spread across his face.

"If all goes according to plan, you won't be able to tell where the seams are." I stared at the wood, trying to see them in all their glory. "I will, but you won't. And it'll be majestic and perfect."

He looped his arms around my waist before I had a chance to step back. "I can't wait." He stared into the depths of my eyes, his gaze flitting between them. "Think it'll be ready before the fifteenth of October?"

"The fifteenth?" I backed away and scanned the pieces. "I thought the renovations wouldn't be done until the end of the month."

Mentally, I was stacking the images of the pieces I still had to carve into my head and placed them on the calendar.

"Good news, they're actually slightly ahead of schedule and are estimating a completion date of mid-month."

I swallowed down a building ball of anxiety. The fifteenth had been my personal date to have it completed, two weeks before its true due date. That was a buffer zone, but to take that away? I glanced around the shop, prioritizing what pieces would be next, and which could wait.

"Will it be a problem? It's okay if you're not going to be ready. Originally, I had said the thirtieth, and it was a date we agreed on."

I forced a weak smile onto my face. "Oh gosh, it'll be fine. It's only a couple of weeks early." Did I sound casual? I hoped so. As it was, I had planned on having it ready early to surprise him. Guess the surprise was on me. "Now I'll just push myself a teeny bit harder and get it done sooner."

Mixing business with pleasure was going to prove a tough

mix. I didn't want to let him down, and he was paying me handsomely, above my typical pricing to make up for part of what he cost me years ago, but still.

"I can pay extra for anything additional you need."

"Like what?" All the materials were paid for and sitting in the shop.

"A sitter, or food delivery, or a steady stream of coffees." There was a slight curve to the right side of his lip when he spoke and a reassuring rub of his hand on my arm.

"I'll be fine. It'll be done. My word is my bond." I sighed and gestured to the house. "I should get back inside."

"Oh, of course."

Walking from the shop to the backdoor was only fifty feet at most, so it surprised me when I could hear banging and crashing sounds. Sprinting, I ran to the back door and yanked it open, taking the four stairs in two, and running to the source of the noise. Vera's room.

She was throwing things in a full-blown tantrum.

I ran in and ducked as a Barbie came at me. I grabbed her and pulled her to the bed, wrapping my arms around her tight. "It's okay. It's okay."

She fought against the restraint, twisting and turning and yelling so loud I worried she may hurt my eardrums in addition to her own.

"It's okay," I repeated and searched her ears.

No hearing aid to be seen.

Her head tipped back, and she roared to the ceiling. This was her frustrated cry. It happened on occasion, where she'd just lose control of herself and the situation and act out. But she hadn't tossed so many of her Barbies before; her room looked as if a tornado had blown through.

After a few minutes of punctuated screaming, and a few kicks to the shins, she finally collapsed breathlessly into my arms, and I held her cradled body tight to mine. I stroked her hair, and pressed her limp hand to my throat, humming so she could feel it. Eventually, she stopped crying and opened her reddened eyes.

"Oh, momma," her lips moved but barely a sound escaped.

"I'm here." My hand brushed down the length of her arm, and I held my hand over hers.

Continuing to hold her close, I waited until she'd calmed down enough, knowing it was safe to put her into her pajamas and tuck her into bed. I stayed beside her, stroking her hair and rubbing her back, until she'd fallen asleep. Resigned that she had truly drifted into a deep sleep, I stepped through the minefield of a room that needed tackling first thing in the morning before school to locate her hearing aids. I needed full light for that.

Mentally exhausted, I ventured out to the kitchen.

"Everything okay?"

Holy shit, I'd forgotten David was still around. "Um, yeah. Surprised you're still here."

"I couldn't leave without first making sure you were both okay. Is Vera going to be all right?" He rose and met me at the counter, handing me a cup of tea. "Sorry, I saw the kettle and the tea bags. Hope you don't think I overstepped?"

"No, that's very sweet of you. Thanks." I took my mug over to the table and collapsed into the chair. "Vera will be fine. Just an episode."

He sat across from me with a mug of black tea, although it looked like he added a splash of milk. "It sounded intense."

I could only imagine how it appeared to someone not in the know; probably like a spoiled brat throwing a tantrum because they didn't get their way, which wasn't at all what had happened.

"Vera has moments of losing her cool. Not a full-blown temper tantrum but no doubt, it looks that way. She'd been overstimulated and was exceptionally over tired, and she didn't have her hearing aid in, so she blew her lid when her world went completely silent." I shrugged. "It's not the first time and it won't be the last time. She started school last week and well, it's been a bit of an adjustment with new wake-up schedules and then the whole school…"

Just thinking of waking her tomorrow to catch the bus sent a shiver down my spine. Hopefully, her exhausted sleep was a solid one and she awoke ready to sparkle like she typically did.

Deep down though, I berated myself. I shouldn't have left her when I knew she was already stretched thin.

I wrapped my hands around the mug. It was warm, but not hot, so the tea had been ready for a while. "Thank you again for this."

He tipped his back. "You're welcome. Figured you need it."

"About what I said earlier, with you staying for a little fun." I stared into my tea, swirling it, and watching the few bubbles swish around.

"You're not in the mood." He covered my hand. "It's okay."

I looked into his eyes. "Thank you."

"It's nothing."

"But it is. I'm a whole package, and I appreciate you being patient with it. With me."

"We all do the best we can, and you're doing a great job."

"Doesn't feel like it some days." It wasn't self-pity though, but it was the truth.

However, I also knew at the end of the day, we were okay. We weren't starving, she was always dressed and taken care of, and had a safe place to live.

I gulped down the lukewarm tea and rose, setting my mug into the well of the sink.

As much as I wanted him to stay, I couldn't kick him out either. The company was nice. Even just the sharing of space between two adults.

David finished off his tea and set his mug beside mine. "Is there anything I can do for you? Give you a back rub or a foot massage?"

179

"Both of those sound mighty heavenly, but I really need to search her room for her hearing aid. I don't know if it fell out or if she threw it." I prayed it fell out. If she threw it and it connected with a wall or something, it could stop working, and right now, I didn't have enough money for a fresh set. She'd need to use an older pair that weren't as good.

"I can help."

"And I appreciate that, truly, but I think it's best if we say goodnight." A dull ache formed.

"I understand." He grabbed my hand and lifted it to his mouth, brushing a kiss across my knuckles. "If there's anything you need, please let me know."

I nodded. "Can I take you up on the foot rub on another day?"

"Absolutely." He took the lead and walked to the back door.

I followed him down and stood on a stair, eye level with him. I leaned closer and kissed him, a sweet kiss, more on the friendly side, rather than one that would lead to a healthy amount of soul-fulfilling sex. No point in getting him fired up for something he couldn't have tonight.

"Good night."

He kissed me back. "Goodnight."

I lingered at the door, watching him slowly saunter away. Locking it, I climbed the stairs to the main floor and gazed through the blinds as he pulled out of my driveway.

Chapter Seventeen

With a new deadline on my hands, I poured every extra minute I had into working on David's mural, and I'd like to say I was making progress, but the reality was, I felt like it was one step forward and two steps back. I had that happen once on another project, yet somehow, it all clicked together at the last minute, so I was holding out hope the same magic would happen with David's mural, although it certainly wasn't looking that way. Even after two weeks.

In the meantime, I followed in Fran's footsteps and met with Lily Morris, an internet genius according to my little sister.

We were set up at Sylvia's Bakery, each of us with a homemade freshly baked goodie and a warm mug of herbal tea.

Lily sat in her chair, turning slightly to the right to accommodate her growing belly.

"When are you due?" I sat across from her.

"Six more weeks. This pregnancy was so much harder than Henry's."

"How old is your son?"

She produced her phone and flashed me a picture. He was a cute, cherubic boy with huge doe-like eyes. "He just turned three."

"Oh, right. Francesca had mentioned something about that since he's coming to her dayhome for a few visits."

"Yeah. It'll just make it easier on me to run some errands, see the midwife, and maybe catch a nap on occasion."

I chuckled, remembering how tired I got with Vera near the end of my pregnancy. "Been there, done that."

She tugged on her long blond braid. "How old are yours?"

"Oh, just the one, and she'll be seven soon."

"Ah, a fun age, so I'm told. There's a wee bit of independence. My niece is nearing that age. A little more precocious, but mainly sweet overall. Three is just plain ole terrible."

I laughed harder. "I called it the *throttle me threes*."

"Is four any better?"

I shook my head. "I wish I could say yes, but… Well, it did get better, eventually."

Lily gave me a warm smile. "So there's hope?"

"Lots of it." I crossed my legs and leaned into the back of my seat. "However, enjoy every minute when you can, the bad and the good. It goes by so ridiculously fast."

"I'll try." She nodded and gave her belly a solid rub as she shifted. "Well, I'm sure you didn't want to get together to discuss motherhood, so how can I help you? Francesca said maybe you needed help with your website?" She pulled an iPad from her bag and turned it on, opening a browser.

"Well sort of, although my website is workable, it's pretty basic. I'd love to add a shop portion and get sales set up that way with whatever I can post."

"Like an Etsy shop?"

"Yes, but I'd rather not pay the high listing fees, and do it myself."

"I totally understand." She tapped the screen and loaded my website address, scrolling through it, although it wasn't very big. I didn't have much on there. "You're right, it's pretty basic. I can jazz it up and add in a storefront too. You want people to pay ahead?"

"Yes."

She listed a few online payment merchants, but only a couple sounded familiar. Being a cash-only business at the markets, I wasn't familiar with most of what Lily was talking about. She pulled out a pad of paper and jotted down some numbers, circling one, and turning the paper in my direction to make it easier to read.

The price was fair.

"I can work with that to build a proper website." I inhaled sharply. "But the real reason I wanted to employ your services was to work on removing a few things off the internet." I rolled my top lip between my teeth.

"Like removing your name and picture from the web?" She leaned closer and rested both her forearms on the table.

I tipped my head from side to side. "Sort of."

Glancing around the bakery, we were pretty much alone. The only other people in the place were staff, with Libby being one, but she was busy working and putting treats into a box.

"Years ago, I left some negative reviews for a place, and I want to remove them all." I stared at the screen where a picture of Chloe's artwork was displayed on my website. "I created various accounts to leave them, something like ten, fifteen, maybe twenty different ones. If I gave you access to the accounts, are you able to go in and reverse search somehow and remove all the postings tied to that name?"

Her eyes widened for a fraction of a second, and then she rubbed her belly. "I should be able to, but they may not all go away. A lot of sites have cached files and even if I did remove your posting, there would still be a footprint there. It's a little outside my capabilities because you're talking about sending take-down notices to companies, and where most will likely honour your request for removal, there will be some who will refuse without payment or court order."

"Shit." I really wanted to wipe it all away. Thought it would be just as easy to wipe out as it had been to post. Oh, why had I been so mean? "So, there's no way?" Crushed, I sagged into my seat and rested my elbows on the table.

"We could try removing a review, and then reaching out to Google to de-index it so remnants won't appear in search results."

"That sounds… Pricey."

She nodded ever so slightly. "There are entire companies devoted to reputation management, but yeah, they'll cost you a lot. Although I'd be cheaper, I'd also be less effective since this is outside of my normal marketing and design forte."

Of course, that's how everything naturally went as far as I was concerned. I could post all I wanted but removing them all was going to take all the extra income I had coming in to clean it all up, likely putting me into further debt, rather than coming out ahead. Why I had been so foolish? Once should've been enough, but noooo, I had to keep at it; like picking a healing wound. Keep picking at the scab until it bled, and once it had scabbed again, pick at it some more.

I was a major idiot. And Birch Bay Burgers became the metaphorical punching bag when I ate his spoiled food, which made me violently ill, and nearly took away the baby I never thought I'd ever have, and then I got fired from a job paying me under the table so I lost my living accommodations on top of that.

But did it help? Nope. Now I was going to be back in debt to fix up something I should've just let go years ago.

"Let me see what I can do. What's the name of one account?" With the pen in her hand, she was ready to scratch down whatever information I could give her.

"Off the top of my head, I don't know. I have some of them

written down at home somewhere."

"Passwords and all?" Her eyes narrowed.

"Yeah, think so." But I wasn't so sure. It's not like I knew at that time I'd need to keep the information for deletion years later.

"It's not a safe thing to keep your passwords written down, unless it's in a password protected app."

"They're not." I wasn't even sure where the piece of paper was that had the emails and passwords listed.

She grabbed her pastry and took an eye-rolling good bite. "Eric brings these home every week, and I swear, they get better tasting each time. Damn, I love this bakery."

"They are addictive." I took a bite of mine as well.

"Anyway, back to your dilemma. How far back are we talking here? Like a few weeks, months? Are they on social media accounts?"

"Yes, several social media accounts, and I can remove those, but I'd like to make sure everything on the net is wiped out, so it could never be traced back to me."

"As if that account never existed?"

"Exactly."

"Well, here's the thing, whatever you put on there is on there forever. Someone could've taken a screenshot."

My face fell, and I had to lift it off the table. "For real?"

"What do you want off the web so bad?" She wiped the corner of her mouth with her napkin and took a sip of her herbal tea. "If I'm going to be hired, I will have to know anyway."

I glanced around again, my gaze darting around to the staff. No one was within earshot. "Reviews I've left on a company."

"That's not so bad. Everyone leaves reviews, it's helpful to the company."

"Not when they are negative."

"But not libelous?"

I tipped my head to the side, not understanding.

"Slander is spoken, libel is written."

"No, everything I wrote was true. I got food poisoning from a product he sold. Although it's his word against mine, I was hospitalized for a few days since I was also pregnant at the time." I stared at the crumbs gathering on the plate. "Normally, I wouldn't be so bothered with having left the bad reviews, but I'm dating the owner of the place now, and I'd rather not have him find out it was me leaving the nasty reviews."

The doorbell rang out, and my focus jumped over to an older couple stomping their way in, dropping their umbrellas into the stand by the door. They looked familiar, but I couldn't place them.

"Oh wow."

"Right?" I picked at a hangnail. "I don't want to ruin our relationship when it's just getting started."

"Well, I'm going to do some digging and see what I can remove. Do you remember where you left the reviews?" She bounced the pen between her fingers.

"If I knew that, I'd start removing them myself, but I don't remember. Definitely his restaurant, but maybe Yelp? Google? Any place where I could. Social media sites. And all under a myriad of different user accounts, emails, and screen names." Damn, I had been ruthless back then; at least recently, I'd kept it narrowed down to a couple of places.

"How many weeks back do you want me to go?"

"Years?"

"I'm sorry?" She nearly choked.

"You'd need to go back seven years." I took a sip and turned away from her wild-eyed expression. Now I was really feeling guilty for my behaviour.

"Okay," Lily finally said, splitting the word into two distinct syllables. "That's going to add up my time."

I hung my head, feeling the full weight of my vengeance. The tires on my truck should last through the winter, so I could set that bill aside, but Vera needed new hearing aids, so I didn't dare touch the savings I'd been slowly accumulating.

"I know. Can we do a payment plan?"

Lily tapped on her device and pulled up a fresh screen. "Of course. I'll send you the contract. Fill in everything you can, adding in any relevant information, and I'll start as soon as you pay the deposit. Depending on how long this takes me, I'll be able to throw in a full website upgrade for free."

"Thank you, I appreciate that."

It was going to cost me a pretty penny now, way more than the additional price I'd built into David's cost, but it would be worth it if he never discovered the truth. I wouldn't be able to live with myself if he did. Now to start listing all the social media websites I'd posted on, all the possible emails used, as surely those were tucked into some sort of e-file, hopefully, maybe. And pray that I could get this all cleaned up without David having never known it was me.

Chapter Eighteen

I parked the truck in front of Birch Bay Burgers and unloaded my folding flat deck dolly, putting a cut piece of carpet overtop the base. Today, I was delivering the seven booth pieces, and collecting the rest of the payment for them. I had warned David I was coming but hadn't said when.

It had been more than a week since I'd seen him, as he snuck over one night after I'd tucked Vera into bed. Since Fran had been hanging around, nothing more than a foot rub had happened, but I was hoping for a little more than that tonight. We were going to go and check out the new brewery in Stewart Surf, and I couldn't be more excited. It was the one-month anniversary of our first date.

I parked the dolly outside the main doors and went inside. The dining room was coming along beautifully, and with the changes slowly sweeping across from one side to the other, the whole place was looking more grown up.

"Can I help you?" The hostess asked as I approached the stand.

"I'm looking for David." I scanned the area and didn't see him in my sights.

"He's just having a brief staff meeting. Once he's done, I can have him come out. I'll take you to your seat." She grabbed a menu and started walking away.

"No. He's commissioned me to build some artwork, and I'm here to deliver part of it."

"Oh." She set her menu down in a huff. "All deliveries need to go through the back door."

"I'm not a food delivery." I pointed out the door in case I wasn't clear. "I have the artwork. On a dolly. Outside."

She narrowed her eyes and a confused expression knit her brows together.

"Tell you what, you tell David that Erin is here, and I'll be out front. Okay?"

"Okay."

I waited for her to move, or blink, or something, but she just stood there.

"Should I write it down? And you can hand him a note?" I started digging through my purse as she still hadn't moved. "You know what, I'll just text him."

"That would be easier."

I nodded, and sent a quick message to David, explaining I

191

knew he was in a meeting, but when he was done, to meet me outside.

It didn't take long until he made long strides across the parking lot in my direction. He greeted me with a panty-melting kiss, making me even more excited for tonight's date.

"Hey," I breathed out when we came up for air. "Happy one-month anniversary."

"Hey, same to you." However, his eyes were tight, and his smile softened the wrinkles that had formed.

"Everything okay? Did you have a rough morning?"

"Just a quick staff meeting. Had to fire a guy."

"Ah, I'm sorry."

"Well, if they don't do the job properly that I'm paying them to do, I help them to the door." His shoulders squared and his whole body seemed to stiffen.

"Well, I hope I can cheer you up a little right now. I have your pieces. The ones for the booths. Figured they were done, and you can have them hung up whenever you're ready." I wrapped my hand around the dolly handle and started pushing it back toward the main doors.

"Let me, and you grab the doors. I know where to put these."

And just like that, he had control and guided us into the restaurant. He drove the cumbersome dolly toward the area tarped in polyfilm. He pulled back the opening and ushered me in.

The new and improved seating area was almost complete. Three booths, which each held four customers comfortably, extended out on either side of a huge six- or eight-person booth in the corner.

"All we need to do is wash everything down, install the seats, hang the artwork, and this area is ready to go." He stepped back to the dolly and held the film door open. "Let's put these here, and the guys can install them tomorrow."

"Don't you want to look at them?" I grabbed one of the frames I'd wrapped in bubble wrap and pulled it back. "All the hanging instructions are included in the envelope."

He took a brief look at it and nodded. "Looks great. I knew you'd do a good job."

"Thanks." I tipped my head to the side, wondering why he was being so wooden.

"Oh, I'll e-transfer you the rest of the payment for these. Can you send me an invoice?" He popped his head out and scanned the dining room, which was hard to see through the opaque film.

"Of course." I reached for his hand, and he shook it free from mine.

"Not here."

"But the kiss outside."

"That wasn't in here." He didn't raise his voice. In fact, it stayed even without a hint of emotion. It was bizarre. "Listen, I'm sorry. I have a ton of paperwork to do with this guy, and I need to get on it."

I tried not to be hurt, but the ache blooming in my chest was hard to avoid.

"Send me the completed invoice for these, and I'll add it to my to-do list."

"Okay." I stared at the dolly and started unloading it.

"I promise I'll be better afterward. I just need to get through this, okay?"

I nodded and stacked another booth piece beside the first one.

"I'll see you later? Pick you up at six sharp?"

"Yeah. That's fine." I didn't look at him as I unloaded another piece.

David stood three, unmoving. "Are you okay?"

"Of course."

"It's the PDA thing, isn't it?" He sighed and ran a hand through his hair. "I just don't show any signs of affection at work. Like none at all. Can't let anyone think I have a soft side, I prefer the tough, no-nonsense business side."

"Having a soft side doesn't make you a bad person, David."

"No. But I get better responses out of my staff when I'm a little hard-edged."

I snorted and tore my gaze away. "If you say so."

He reached for my hand but thought better of it. "See you tonight. You'll be ready?"

"Absolutely."

By the time six o'clock rolled around, I had fed my daughter and sister, cleaned the kitchen, and had my bag packed by the back door. There was no sign of David. I'd texted, checking in to make sure everything was okay, and it went unanswered. Having only been the recipient of a firing once, I knew the emotional distress it did to the person being fired, but would it do the same to the person doing the firing? Maybe that's what had happened to David?

"I'm going out to the shop," I said to anyone who was listening.

Francesca barely waved, she and Vera were grossly engaged in a head-to-head match of Candy Land.

"I'll let you know when I'm leaving." I walked out to the shop.

Since I was dressed in relatively nice clothes for our *Brewing under the Stars* event, I wasn't going to work, but I could attend to some paperwork. Shrugging out of my sweater, I sat at my makeshift desk and scrolled through the open spreadsheet file I had going with the updated email accounts I had created, along with possible passwords, a myriad collection of hashtags I'd used, and the social media accounts I thought were tagged to each email address.

What was once a small tree, was turning into a giant forest, and I was so fucked. So far, I had accounted for roughly seventeen email accounts and had recently asked for password resets, since I couldn't remember the stupid things. A smarter person would've used the same password for all the bogus accounts, but that hadn't been me apparently. The list was growing longer by the day, and each email address I discovered pushed shame deeper in my shoulders and pounded against my brain. I had been beyond stupid to go to such lengths.

I printed it out and set it on the desk so I could give it to Lily.

Needing to beat myself up further, I opened David's invoice for the booth pieces and double-checked his invoice against Chloe's, feeling more guilt as I held the two papers in my hand and compared. Each booth piece was slightly smaller than Chloe's, yet the price was vastly higher. A giant increase, in fact, multiplied by seven.

A deep current of shame rivered through my soul. How petty was I? I was the lowest order of the human race to keep exacting revenge on a guy and a business years after the fact.

With a heavy sigh, I set the papers down.

I wandered over to the mural and gave it a solid look over. My pricing on it had been marginally higher, however, now that I knew the guy, I was going to put in extra effort and make this my big deal. Every artist had that one piece, the one they put their heart and soul into, well, this was going to be mine. My magnum opus.

The doorbell chimed on my phone, and a moment later, David knocked and entered the shop.

Naturally, he looked stunning and had changed out of his dress shirt, opting for a nice pair of pants and a looser-fitting button-up. Still, he was dressed like a million dollars.

I met him halfway and gave him a solid once-over. The warmth had returned to his eyes, and there was a spring in his step.

"Hello, gorgeous."

"Hey." My heart fluttered like a teenaged girl, which was crazy because I was twice her age.

"Sorry I'm late. I had a few last-minute things to handle and then we were short-staffed, so I had to step in—"

"David, it's okay." I reached up and kissed him. The way we had started in the parking lot of his restaurant.

He swept a hand down my cheek. "Well, you keep kissing me like that, and we will really be late getting to the brewery."

I wiggled my brows. Maybe I didn't care too much about that. All I wanted was to spend time with David, that could be here, there, anywhere. I wasn't picky.

"Let's go." I held his hand. "My bag is at the back door, and I'll just say goodnight to the girls."

We walked to the shop door.

"Oh, let me grab my sweater."

It was hanging on the chair by my desk.

"I'll get it," David said, already there before I could stop him.

As if in slow motion, he scanned the desk, his focus lasering on the stack of printouts scattering on top of my desk. My heart plummeted to the floor.

"What the hell is this?"

Chapter Nineteen

flicked off the iPad and dropped it onto the stack of papers, trying to cover the most damaging one of them all. "It's nothing."

"It has my name on it."

My mind raced at a thousand miles per hour. "It's your updated invoice. I was just making sure I didn't miss anything."

He lunged for the papers, flipping through them, as his eyes grew wider with each flip.

"You know, you have no right to be going through my things." I snatched them out of his hands. "I don't show up at your place of work and rifle through your invoices on cheese and steaks."

"Why was Chloe's piece so much cheaper, when it was larger?"

"Different materials; her's was cheaper wood." It wasn't a lie.

His focus remained on the paper, until finally a few thick,

soul-crushing moments later, he looked me in the eyes. "Did you gouge me on the mural too?"

I folded the papers in half. "No, I didn't gouge you."

He stood there staring, eyes twitching into a slight narrow, and I suddenly felt like one of his employees about to be fired; the darkness in his eyes wasn't one of happiness and joy.

"But I did raise the price. Slightly." Saying it didn't make me feel any better though.

"What? Why?" His gaze narrowed into thin slits, like his lips.

"Because—"

"Because I'm a rich business owner and you figured you stick it to the man like everyone else?" His tone was as ugly as his words, and it ruffled my feathers.

"No, that's not it."

"You need to give me something Erin."

Suddenly my name didn't have the usual sweet ring to it. "I don't have to explain anything to you, and I especially don't need to explain my business dealings."

"Maybe not your business dealings, but you can explain why the guy you're dating is paying a higher price than your friends did."

I needed to circle back to all he was saying to truly understand where his emotions were blowing out from, but my mouth spoke before my brain thought it all the way through. "Are you asking for a discount?"

"Not at all. But I expect fairness."

"Fairness? You *expect* fairness." I leaned forward, feeling like my eyes were going to bug out of my head. "Let's talk about fairness, shall we? Years ago, I ate in your restaurant, back when you had a takeout option. Ordered myself a little grilled chicken wrap. I was six months pregnant, and I figured after working a double shift at the diner, I'd treat myself to a meal; the kind I didn't have to prepare nor clean up after. However, when I got home and started eating it, it didn't taste right. The chicken was raw, a gross pink colour, and despite that, was hidden in a thick slathering of sauce."

He held his breath.

"I got ill that night, violently ill. I called in sick to work the next day as I hadn't stopped throwing up. After thirty-seven hours of non-stop violent heaving, I went to the hospital, and they admitted me, well us, for dehydration and to keep an eye on my baby. Eventually, I stopped throwing up, but I'd missed two days of work. The boss didn't like that, didn't think the reasoning for my absence was acceptable, and fired me. Can you believe that? Now I had no job."

He stood there, the expression on his face softening for just a touch, but his whole body remained as stiff as a statue.

"I reached out to your restaurant and spoke to the manager. I explained the situation, and he laughed, *you* laughed over my distress, and said there was no proof. It was my word against yours and said if I was so god-damn concerned to hire a lawyer. Then you hung up on me."

He took a half step back, the shadows darkening on his face.

"I relied on the tips and that shitty under-the-table wage to pay my rent, but without that job, I couldn't afford to pay said rent. My landlord, bless her heart, gave me a bit of grace, but no one wants to hire a six-month pregnant lady. Trust me, I looked. Everywhere." My heart was constricting as I remembered that horrible time in my life, and although my breath felt like it was losing steam, the verbal diarrhea hadn't slowed down. "I think you can see where this is heading."

There was a light nod. "You lost your home."

"Yep, sure did. All because of an uncooked chicken wrap. That came from your business. So, let's discuss fairness, shall we?"

He inhaled sharply, blinked a few times, and rubbed his temples aggressively. "Are you the one who called the health board?"

"Multiple times, and I wasn't even sorry." My head shook with that and I crossed my hands over my chest. Because I wasn't. Of that, I did not have a smidgen of remorse.

He swiped his hands down his face, his eyes widened, and his nostrils flared. "Holy shit. Are you responsible for the…" Without hesitation, his eyes scanned my desk, grabbing another set of fresh from the printer papers. "These email addresses and social media accounts… Customers? Or pissed off reviewers?"

Oh shit. A coolness wrapped around me, taking away the heat from the anger surge. I wasn't going to try to take the papers from him. Now I just didn't care.

"It was revenge, David. I was mad. You wouldn't give me any compensation. Even a couple of hundred dollars would've helped. Instead, you laughed at me and told me to get a lawyer, although you were pretty sure I didn't have a leg to stand on."

He threw the papers onto my desk, except for one. "But yet, somehow you decided to keep screwing me over. For years. That's just … I don't even have the words for that. Damn, Erin. Talk about overreacting. Talk about being malicious. Jesus, I thought you were a nice person."

The truth stabbed a million little jagged knives into my soul. "I am now, but I can admit then, I wasn't. I was so angry. I had to protect my baby. I had to fight. Yes, I overreacted, but I almost lost my baby. I was scared and demoralized, and feeling like nothing in my life was going right."

"And I was your punching bag."

Yes, it was true. He was the only one I could fight. As it was, the diner I was working for went belly up a few months later. Who else could I go after? If I had eaten anywhere else that night…

"Wow. You think you know someone." He shook his head and rocked back and forth. "So all this time, you were just exacting some kind of sick revenge on me? Up charging me for something that happened years ago because the hate reviews you've been leaving *for years* weren't enough?" The words *for years* hung in the air like a glowing, neon sign.

"That was before I got to know you."

"Oh, okay, so my heart and affections also filtered into this too, did they? Was making me care for you part of your plan? That I'd finally found someone who I respected, and it was all a lie? I was just revenge?" His words were like pointed knives, each one zooming through the growing distance between us and stabbing me right in the heart.

"It's not like that at all. Once I got to know you, I started deleting the reviews and trying to erase all the—"

He threw the papers onto the desk, and they floated in different directions. "You know what, we're done. Keep your mural. Keep the down payment too." He stormed over to the door in five long strides. "But know this, I won't leave a bunch of negative reviews on your website, and I won't ever upcharge you, should you find yourself in my restaurant. That's not who I am. This is all..." His words sputtered as his hands flew around. "So unforgivable."

He slammed the door so hard I was sure downtown Cheshire Bay felt the earth move.

Chapter Twenty

I sent a text to Francesca, letting her know I wasn't going anywhere tonight, but I was instead staying in the shop to finish a project and needed to be left alone. However, as I stood there feeling stupid and heartbroken, and crying so hard I couldn't see straight, I wasn't sure which project to tackle – the review takedown or the mural.

Feeling the rage fire up in me wasn't good for calm, logical thinking, so I decided to channel that energy into building the mural.

Headphones on to drown out my thoughts, I dove into the project. My first break came near midnight, as my hands were stiff, and my back was achingly sore. I needed to take a quick mental break, and a walk was in order. I stepped outside the shop and inhaled the fresh scent. The streets had pools of water, and the streetlights reflected a little sheen.

I strolled down my street and turned left, heading toward downtown, only intending on going far enough to clear my head and infuse some fresh energy into my weary soul. I walked to the park, and spying a bench, sat upon it, the wet on the seat soaking into my pants. The events of the evening replayed in my head. I shouldn't have been so careless. I should've dropped the vendetta I had years ago, and not given in to Libby's idea of upcharging him, but that wasn't her fault. She wasn't the one who added that to the bill, that had all been on my shoulders, my stupid revenge-seeking shoulders.

David was right, I was a lousy human being. My act had been unforgivable, and the weight of that deception pushed on my heart and soul.

After grabbing an XL coffee from the twenty-four-hour convenience store, I put a little pep in my step and hammered my pace back home, where I poured everything I had into the mural.

By the time the morning light filtered in through the side window, I'd made great progress.

Bleary-eyed, I stumbled into the house and made breakfast. Vera had school, and Fran's dayhome kids would be arriving shortly.

My sister breezed into the kitchen fresh as a daisy, ready to take on the world.

I needed to absorb some of her energy, so I found myself standing closer to her in hopes it would jump over.

"How was last night? You were working pretty hard." She raised her brows as she poured a cup of coffee. "Everything okay?"

I avoided eye contact. "Not at all, but I'm trying to figure out how to fix it."

"Can I help?"

"Only if you can turn back time." I flipped a pancake onto the growing stack and handed it to Fran.

"Yeah, can't do that. So, it's more than guy troubles? Those I'm good at solving."

I rolled my bottom lip between my teeth. "It is guy troubles, but it's complicated, and sex won't fix it."

"You're talking to the mistress of complicated." She added syrup to the table. "How can I help?"

"I don't know. I really screwed up." I relayed what I'd told David, about the food poisoning and losing my rental.

"Wow, that super sucks. If David wasn't going to compensate you, why didn't you reach out to Vera's father, surely he should've had an invested stake in the health of his unborn child?"

A shudder rolled through my body just remembering him. A man-child if ever there was one. The kind of guy who had more desire to have a tooth extracted without pain meds than to have a child, as I sadly learned. A man who broke me when he dismissed me, with his blatant refusal to accept that after his forced intrusion on my personal space he'd fathered a child because I wasn't supposed to be able to get pregnant. He claimed I was a liar and just after him to stir up shit.

"I did reach out, but after the fact. I needed to get back on my feet first." I turned my attention back to the pancakes, a couple of which were quite dark, but not fully burnt when I flipped them over.

"But you know what, that gives me an idea. David asked me to open up, so I think I should tell him about her father."

"Tell me first," Francesca pleaded. "You never talk—"

I covered her mouth as Vera dragged her feet into the kitchen. I wasn't going to say a word about the jerk in front of his child; those were details Vera didn't need to know now or ever. Only one person knew the nitty-gritty details surrounding Vera's father, and Adam had been sworn to secrecy about all nasty details. Not even my parents knew the full truth.

I put the rest of the pancakes onto the plate. "Dig in while they're warm."

Vera grabbed a couple and blew on them, while I went and grabbed her hairbrush. As she ate, I silently styled her hair into two braids. I thought it looked cute, like something Libby would wear, but Vera didn't care for it. She was all about the Rey hairstyle, and all about it coming from her aunt.

"Well, now you look like Ahsoka Tano."

"Who?" I cocked my eyebrow at my sister, who was talking and signing to Vera.

"She's a Jedi Knight. Very tough. No one messes with her."

Vera signed. "Princess?"

Hand flat above her lips, Francesca pulled it away, curling it into a thumbs-up position. "Better."

Vera grabbed the braids and ran her hands along the length of them, a smile building on her sweet cheeks. "Okay. I like."

"Thank you," I mouthed to Fran.

"I want details." She winked and stabbed a stack of pancakes.

The bus honked, and with her backpack and lunch bag, we both walked her to the bus and sent her off to school.

"I need to get to work." I was already two steps closer to the shop.

"But I thought you'd tell me things."

"Not with your charges arriving." I nudged toward the car pulling into the driveway. "See you at supper."

Safe from the interrogation I suspected I hadn't completely avoided, I set to work adding the details to the remaining pieces.

Somehow, by the grace of Francesca's never-ending child-minding and multiple trips to the shop to bring me food and drinks, I completed the mural ahead of schedule, barely. As it was, it was only four days ahead of his amended date. I'd put all my energy and time into it, and I practiced snapping it together to make sure it would work. Getting it apart proved trickier than I expected, but eventually it came apart – with no damage. It truly had become my magnum opus.

Piece by piece I hauled it out to the truck and loaded it into the scratched and weathered bed. Despite my daily attempts, David never returned my text messages nor answered my calls. Since I hadn't wanted to show up at the restaurant unannounced, with no place to put the mural pieces, I made sure to let him know in one of the messages. I wasn't expecting to see him when I arrived.

But he was there, and he was as expectantly silent and unwavering as ever.

As per the instructions from the crew who happened to be there, since I didn't dare ask David, I brought in the first of several pieces and set them in the tarped area, ignoring the pinched expressions of the dining patrons. I'd taken care to lay the wooden slats out in the order they'd need to hang up and included detailed instructions on how to mount everything. Once I walked away, it was in the hands of the renovation company, especially since I wasn't going to collect the rest of the payment and had no intention of following up with David. The business deal was dead. Just like our relationship.

Too many nights I'd cried myself to sleep wondering what I could've done to prevent our split. The only thing was not being a malicious bitch hellbent on revenge. But I didn't know David the person back then, I only knew the manager, whose name I never recalled getting.

Heart aching from hanging out in his restaurant, and somehow feeling he was present yet invisible, tormented me. Every trip to and from the truck, I scanned and scouted, and sighed in great disappointment.

Was he in the dining room talking with his customers? Not on any of the searching I did.

Was he in the kitchen watching his cooks, making sure everything was perfect? Again, I saw no sign on the trips I took.

My best guess was he was avoiding me, plain and simple, and possibly watching me from his office, and that was the one area I gazed up to as I lumbered from the reno area back through the dining room and out the door. My shoulders sagged, and I was curled around my middle more than normal; the weight of being a raging disaster was a tough burden to carry.

When I set the last piece down, I took a final, empty-hearted look around. To my surprise, the booth pieces were already hanging, and dang it, I had to admit they looked great. There was a sense of pride seeing my artwork on display, knowing I had created it with my bare hands and it was hanging for all to see. I'd half expected him to have changed his mind, but then again, based on the cost…

A shadow crossed my left field of view.

David walked around the dining room and stopped a few feet from me. His voice was as chilling as a winter's breeze. "Do you have a minute before you go?"

My mouth was as dry as the desert, and I stiffened in response, but my heart hammered so loudly, I barely heard him. "Of course."

"Come to my office please."

Nodding slowly, I removed my work gloves and gave myself a quick dusting before I followed him through the dining room, in through the kitchen where several staff stopped what they were doing to watch me follow behind like a dog with my tail tucked between my legs. One heavy step at a time, I ambled up the curving stairs.

He sat at his desk, rubbing his temple with his left hand, while he motioned to the door with his right. "You can close that."

My chest tingled and my fingertips turned as cold as the room felt. I sat on the only other chair available, and it was firm and uncomfortable, much like me. A sour taste formed in the back of my mouth. "Before you say anything, I want to apologize."

He cracked his lips apart, but I lifted a finger to stop him.

"I didn't mean for things to get so out of hand with regards to the reviews. That was low, and really, the first couple should've just been enough." My hands clasped together, and a razor-edged lump formed in the back of my throat. "I've hired a service to help in removing those malicious reviews since I can't do it on my own."

"Mmmhmm." He tore his eyes off me just long enough to pick up his phone and type into it.

I tugged at my shirt collar and as I moved my arm, I caught a whiff of myself. Damn. Could he smell my body odor too? Jesus, how embarrassing. A swatch of sweat bloomed across the nape of my neck, tightening and curling the little hairs dangling from my low ponytail.

Clearing my throat, I shifted in my seat. "Yes, I did wrong, and wholeheartedly accept that, however, given the circumstances, I think I deserve some understanding and forgiveness too. I was not myself. And neither were you."

"I see."

Jesus, that was the wrong thing to have said.

Scorn shadowed his face as he aggressively rubbed his beard, and as his eyes burrowed into my soul, which I let him penetrate. I no longer had anything left to hide.

"And for all that, I'm sorry." My breath strangled me, and my voice lost some of its power. "I know my apology means dick in the grand scheme of things, but I'm open to ideas on how to fix that and make things better with you." I broke our connection and focused on the edge of his immaculate desk. My voice fell further, barely audible like a breath in the wind, but somehow it managed to stay together without completely shattering, unlike my heart. "And about the money and the cost difference."

"I'm not even concerned about that."

Did I—What?

I shook my head as I wasn't sure how to respond. I'd mentally played over a dozen different scenarios, but none of them had him saying anything close to not being concerned.

"You brought all the pieces in today?"

I nodded, wondering if I should've brought in Vera's hearing aid as I still wasn't sure I was hearing properly.

"You're what, eighteen days ahead of schedule?"

"Something like that." Closing my arms, and trapping my sweaty scent firmly in my armpits, I inhaled a lung full of fresh air, and with it a little more confidence. "I finished before the originally scheduled completion, and just a few days prior to the amended version."

I hadn't slept much over the past few days and every single minute I wasn't with Vera, I had been in the shop.

"It's all there?"

"Complete with instructions for the reno guys to snap it all into place. Easier to put together than furniture from Ikea."

At least that caused a weak smile to start.

The desk rattled and he retrieved an envelope, sliding it in my direction. "Payment in full."

The thick, standard-sized envelope sat there, holding my rapt attention. There was a lot of money on the table, and it was needed. There was so much it could pay for.

But I couldn't. I didn't have much, but I had my integrity.

Begrudgingly, my heart plummeting into my stomach, I pushed it back, however, my finger lingered on the edge for a couple of heartbeats. "I can't accept this."

"You did the job, ahead of schedule, and you worked really hard on it. Take the money. You've earned it."

Once again, the envelope grabbed my attention, almost glowing like a pot of gold at the end of a ray of sunshine.

So. Much. Money. I knew because I had looked at the remainder of the invoice and what was due on the mural; I just never sent it. He'd already paid for the booth pieces in full, and I was going to make do with that.

"Take it. Consider us even now."

That's it? We were even now? I wasn't even going to get a chance to beg to bring us back together?

My heart constricted and my shallow breath shuddered, and I wasn't sure what to say and do. Being *even* wasn't a thought I'd prepared for, because in my mind, we weren't. I screwed up, and I needed to find a way to mend us, but as the envelope was pushed back in my direction, with such a strong finality in his voice, an ache bloomed deep within my soul.

A few minutes ago, I was hot and sweaty, but I suddenly shivered with the chill. "I'm not even close to making things right. Not with you. Not by a long shot."

My new magnum opus was to make sure everything was smoothed over with David, who had been my boyfriend for a brief spell, and make us bigger and better than we had been because, for a small moment in time, it was beyond wonderful. Too many nights since our fight, I curled in my bed and let the tears fall. I missed the shared space with an adult. I missed the connection. I truly missed him.

"It's retribution costs for that horrible night I unintentionally dropped on you. After we had that…" His chest pushed out against the buttons of his shirt. "That fight…" He dropped his gaze back to his phone for a couple of heartbeats. "I came back here and dug through all the old files. The good thing about being a micromanager…" He let the word hang between us with a tiny smirk.

"Is I keep exceptionally detailed files, much longer than the government requires. It turns out there *was* a container of chicken marked and tossed as spoilage around the time you contracted food poisoning."

Had this been announced seven years ago, I might have jumped up and down waving my fists in the air in celebration, but I wasn't about now. Instead, I swallowed and looked him deep in the eyes.

"That's... interesting."

"Back then, as I've told you, I was going through a rough patch, but that doesn't excuse my behaviour as a manager of this restaurant. It took some deep thinking, but I recalled that conversation, and I am regrettably sorry for having laughed at you and said what I said." He hung his head before returning his focus to me. "I should've been the bigger person. A couple hundred dollars would not have bankrupted me the way the situation almost did to you. For that, please accept this payment, with bonus, as me asking for forgiveness for that horrible event."

The money-stuffed envelope just sat there like a lead weight with pointy neon arrows aimed right at it.

"For that callous behaviour, I most decidedly earned a bad review, and I definitely agree it needs to remain."

I'd waited years to hear an apology, but now that it had happened, I wasn't feeling any better. The lump in my throat grew sharp little spikes, and I swallowed it down with a bitter taste of bile.

He pushed the payment toward me. "Please."

"If you insist."

"I do. I can own up to that one, but the others were excessive, mean, and totally out of line."

"Agreed. One hundred percent. And again, for that, I am beyond sorry."

He nodded briefly and rose. "Then that concludes my business with you today." Without another word, he walked over to the door and opened it wide.

My jaw unhinged. My heart stopped beating. My head swam.

"But I'm not finished. Not by a long shot." My breath twisted into a miserable knot of gasps and shallow sounds. "Please. There's more I want to tell you."

The phone buzzed on his desk, but he ignored the vibration. With a soul-crushing escape of air from his lungs, he closed the door and sat in his chair, leaning back as he crossed his legs. "You have five minutes."

Chapter Twenty-One

Five minutes wasn't a lot of time to bare my soul and beg for forgiveness. To show him I wanted him, that I needed him too. My chest tingled as it constricted, and a pricking sensation crawled across the nape of my neck.

I quickly cleared my throat and stared at my laced fingers. "While I had revenge on the brain and had become so narrowly focused I couldn't see straight, there was a reason - I was in a bad place before that happened."

My heart hammered with his full, undivided attention. I hadn't shared my story with anyone but it was time.

"Thing is... My story..." I sighed and crossed my legs, rolling my shoulders in, wondering how far in my timeline I had to go back. "You see, when I was sixteen, I was told there was no way I would ever have a baby. I'll spare you the details on the why, and we'll just leave it at that. Flash forward a few years..."

A flood of adrenaline leaked into my system, setting off all sorts of bells and whistles. Lightheaded, I looked around the room to keep myself in the moment; over to the windows along the carpet's edge, over to the closed door which was going to contain my past to the two souls in the shared space, and over to the man I'd come to adore. I needed to remind myself that David had earned my trust, and I could share this with him. I needed to.

A violent shudder rippled through me as the past flashed in memories.

"Quinn was quite well off, from a long line of wealth and entitlement. He'd met my brother Adam, but I can't remember how they became friends or why." Just picturing that poster boy made my stomach sour. What had I found so intoxicating about him? Looking back now, it must've been the rose-coloured glasses I wore. The hairs lifted on my arms as a cool breeze floated in the air. "Anyway, that part isn't important." My gaze stayed trained on the envelope neither of us had moved yet. "Over a few dates, I felt Quinn and I had a connection. I was wrong. So god-damned wrong." My eyes squeezed shut, not that it removed the images. "One night at a party, I was more than a little drunk and Quinn was more than a little handsy…"

The desk between us shook, and his breath came in rasps.

I lowered my voice and fought to remember how to breathe as I shook my head and rolled tighter into a ball. "Long story short, that night, well, he took… he…" I couldn't even say the words. Or *the* word as it was. The lump in my throat plummeted into my stomach with a sour splash. "The kicker of it all was learning a few weeks later, I wasn't experiencing some sort of early onset menopause. I was pregnant."

More adrenaline pumped at a breakneck speed, and I wanted a hole to open up in the floor and swallow me whole. The ground had vibrated a touch, and as I finally opened my eyes, I saw why – David had quietly moved from behind his desk to sit on the edge beside me. He was close enough that I caught a whiff of his cologne.

I focused on his hands resting on his lap. "A total shock, one that completely blindsided me, especially when I was told I would never – could never – carry a baby. Imagine all the emotions surrounding that."

To learn I was carrying a child I'd never thought I'd have, while also wrapping my head around the way conception occurred… it was mind boggling. I had so many feelings, and I was confused and hurt and surprised. Giving the baby up wasn't an option, and neither was the other possibility. I only had one choice; one I never regretted a day in my life.

My focus stayed trained on the wood grain edging of his desk.

His hand twitched and his breath was laboured, but he made no further movement. He was close enough to touch, if I felt I needed his strength. Just sharing the space with me gave me a comforting push to carry on.

"My family just assumed I was knocked up and that the jerk had abandoned me, until I accidentally ran into him at Adam's bookstore by fluke. I confronted him. I showed him the twenty-two-week ultrasound I carried around in my purse. He said there was no proof it was his, but I knew because he'd been the only person I'd… well, at that time…" I pressed the back of my hand to my mouth to muffle a cry. "Anyway, Adam overheard the whole conversation and closed his shop immediately. There were a lot of tears, a lot of hugs, and a whole whack of angriness, but he always swore me to secrecy. Although I was carrying proof of what happened." I swallowed, the noise ear-shattering in the deadly silence. "I didn't want to go ahead with pressing charges and being run through the mud."

Like a whisper in the wind, he spoke. "That would never happen."

A soft snort blew out, and lightning bolts of anger flashed out. "It happens all the time. The woman has to shoulder all of it; it's her who gets questioned on how much she drank, what she was wearing, and the focus falls to her, not to the guy who, you know… shouldn't have…"

A trembling began in my hands and feet, and I pumped my crossed leg to ward off the feeling. It didn't help.

"Anyway." I inhaled a desperately needed breath of air through my quivering lips. "Adam dealt with him somehow, I never got the full details, and forced him to submit to a DNA test. Guess what?"

"It was his."

"Without a doubt."

"So you pressed charges then?"

I shook my head as heat singed my cheeks. "I wasn't that brave, but I did email him several times to let him know he was the father. I sent copies of the test, but it was radio silence. I didn't expect a free ride, or for him to pony up any money, so I worked double shifts. Joke was on me though. Since I was paid under the table, when I couldn't come into work because I was sick in the hospital and they canned me, I had no recourse for income. I was broke. I lost my apartment on top of it all and moved back in with my parents for a short spell. Sadly, because it was something tangible, you, well not you, but your business, took the brunt of my anger. The baby's father had disappeared, and the restaurant I'd gotten sick at wasn't going to pay my lost wages and therefore help me keep on treading water, I was screwed. Stupidly, I poured my energy into the one thing I could grab onto."

David inhaled sharply. "My restaurant became your metaphorical punching bag."

I slowly scanned up his body, over his rising and falling chest, over his beard, and up into his dark eyes. "Yes."

The air crackled between us, and I wasn't sure if I should continue, wait, or what.

"Keep going, I need to hear the rest," David urged as he rose and swung his chair to roll beside mine. Sitting down, he took my hand into his. "Then what?"

"A few months later, I received a letter, through Adam's

bookshop, from a lawyer's office. In exchange for my silence on the baby's paternity, because it would ruin him and his entitled future…" I rolled my eyes. "He agreed to drop all paternity rights. I had no money to hire a lawyer to contest, but Adam stood by my side, and without my parents knowing, because the details are embarrassing, we filed some sort of counter. Quinn wasn't going to get off that easy."

"And?"

"Long story short, his family transferred a small amount of money to me, which I in turn used a few years later on Vera's house. It helped with a down payment. However, in accepting the bribe I had to agree to leave his name off the birth certificate, and never mention him or his family by name ever again. For that, he had to sign away any rights to Vera, which he did with gusto."

"Oh wow." David leaned back in his chair and thoughtfully rubbed his chin. "That's quite a story. No one knows who the father is?"

I shook my head. "Just Adam."

"Your parents don't even know?"

"They do, sort of, but not really. All they know is I was given a lump payment. They aren't aware of the nitty-gritty details surrounding the circumstances." I wasn't proud of that, but I was a grown adult and for the most part, I was doing the best I could. "Vera and I will never have to worry about him ever again."

"But why did you continue to keep going after me? That's

what I don't understand. Yes, I caused a cascade of events to happen, but you got the…" He grimaced. "Settlement from him, so the money wasn't a factor."

"The money came after the fact. Many months afterward."

However, no reason could explain my constant barrage of negative reviews. In my life of uncertainty, it was the only thing I could control, and really, even that was an illusion.

"I'm so sorry." I hung my head as my shattering heart, under the deepest pressure, threatened to blow apart. "I know it doesn't make up for it, but I'm trying to clean up the damage I caused. Just please, tell me what I can do."

Rising, he rifled through a neatly stacked pile of folders, pulling out one with an orange tab sticking out as he sat back in his chair. "Well, as disgusted as I was to learn it was you with a vendetta against my company, I did some research."

I curled my hands into tight little fists and held my breath.

"Your attacks, unfortunately for your goal, did not affect my sales." He leaned back, his shoulders relaxing. "I compared sales from the year previous and the year following. They were within normal accepted ranges."

My breath whooshed out in one fell swoop and hot tears blurred my view. "I can't tell you how happy I am to hear that. Now. Especially since I've met you and taken a liking to you."

A small curve turned his lips upward and a sparkle returned to his eyes. "And I suppose I should thank you."

"How come? What for?" I swiped at the fallen tears.

"I now keep the cleanest kitchen in all Cheshire Bay, and my annual inspections are A+, and surprise inspections pass with flying colours. I run a tight ship, but everyone is happy."

"Then it's a good thing you're a micromanager."

"Thank you." His smile deepened, and he twisted to the side, putting his leg atop his knee. "It is good to be in total control."

"And now? We're good?" I hesitated as an idea popped into my head. A way to fully make things better, or at least try.

"Business wise, I think we've reached an agreement. You accept the cash for the full payment of the mural, which I can't wait to see all put together, and drop the other negative reviews, and I think that yes, we'll be fine on that end." He lifted the heavy envelope and placed it in my hand. "Please, take it. Don't make me give it to your sister to give to you." There was a glint in his eye.

"Personally? What happens between us now?" I dropped my gaze, not wanting to see rejection. Hearing it was going to be hard enough.

"I'm not sure. You were one to tell me trust was earned, not freely given."

This speech I was prepared for. "Taking out the business aspect of our relationship, and not knowing really who the other was back then, if we base things on how things have been progressing over the past few weeks, what would you say happens now?"

He shook his head and dropped his leg, squaring up his

shoulders. "Honestly, I don't know. I like you, I really do, and I like your daughter."

My hand flashed up, putting a stop to what was heading my way. The word *but* was coming like a red-hot knife, ready to wound.

"Before you tell me it'll never happen, can you have lunch with me?"

He narrowed his eyes and casually glanced at his watch. "I don't know, Erin, I really don't know."

"Please. Like a date. Like we're starting over." An idea splashed across my brain, the details emerging at lightning speed.

He hesitated, and I took that as a positive sign.

"Give me five minutes, and meet me downstairs?"

Chapter Twenty-Two

I zipped down the office stairs, through the kitchen, and headed over to the hostess, telling her what I wanted to do. Then I ran to the bathroom, freshened up, and made myself more presentable before walking back to the hostess and greeting her once again.

She led me to the patio overlooking the bay.

"This isn't opened back up to the public yet, so you'll have some privacy, and it's one of Mr. Dean's favourite places to sit."

There was a lone table set up with a deep navy tablecloth and a centerpiece with string lights giving it a nice glow. Placements were set for two. The hostess outdid herself with my request.

"Can I get you a drink?" She pulled out my chair for me and ushered me in.

"I'm good. The water here will be enough, but please bring whatever David's favourite drink is." My mouth was parched, so I took a drink to moisten it.

The glass was chilled, and the coolness seeped into my hands, making me colder than I already was.

David joined me a few minutes later, looking slightly refreshed and smelling like he'd just applied a new spritz of cologne. "Sorry, just a little something I need to take care of. You forgot this."

The envelope fell with a dull thud in front of me.

"You've absolutely earned it."

"Thank you." I cleared my throat and pointed to his seat. "Now that the business portion of the meeting has been concluded, let's get to the heart of the matter, shall we?"

The door behind David opened and the waiter set down two plates of food. The one he sat in front of his boss was a steak sandwich, with a healthy side of fries and a Greek salad. The one he sat in front of me was a chicken Caesar wrap.

David's eyes grew bigger. "Seriously?"

Nodding, I forced a semblance of a smile to spread out my lips, as I crossed my legs and let my foot bounce to the race of my heart. "Alright, let's dig in."

David set his napkin across his lap as I lifted the chicken wrap to my mouth. It smelled amazing and looked just as good. The chicken was there, among the lettuce, strips of red pepper, and shredded cheese with bits of bacon, but until I took a bite of it, I had no idea what to expect. Everything was good, right?

Hesitantly, with his wild-eyed gaze upon me, I pushed the top of the wrap into my mouth and chomped down. Flavour by flavour,

I sorted out the bits of food until I tasted the Caesar dressing. Biting the bullet, I bit into the chicken. It was cooked, almost too much cooked, but it was good, edible.

Heart pounding and my breathing just as fast, I set the wrap down and wiped the corners of my mouth.

"Wow." David leaned forward, eagerly awaiting my response.

"It was good. Cooked." I added, swallowing it down. It wasn't my favourite, not by far, but I was no longer going to be intimidated by eating at David's restaurant. "A new review will reflect the tastiness."

"You don't have to eat anymore." He reached for my hand. "I can't believe you'd do that. Why?"

"Because, David, I like you and this was a small step to making amends." I stared deep into his eyes, searching for the passage that would lead me to his soul once again, and held still.

"Well, I like how you call me on my bullshit and micromanaging, and the way you are with Vera, and how you put aside your own needs for her."

I shook my head. "Every mother does that, it doesn't make me special."

"But it does. And it's one of the many things about you I like."

One of the many things, I repeated mentally. All was not lost. I clutched at my chest as a fresh jolt of energy zipped through.

"You know what I think?"

I wished I did.

His chest expanded with a deep breath. "I think every person is entitled to a do-over. Whether in business," he pointed to the two plates of mostly untouched food, "or pleasure." He waggled a finger between him and me. "Do you agree?"

"For the most part, yes." There were some things and some people who would never be given a second chance. Ever.

"Do you think we can start over? Now, with the whole business arrangement behind us, can we just be two people who met and found they really enjoyed the other's company? Two people who understand the other on a level most never know about and who connect so well intellectually, that," he leaned closer to whisper in my ear, even though we were all alone, "the sex is mind-blowingly awesome."

Heat rushed to my cheeks at a breakneck speed, washing away any remnants of chill. Just whispering the words ignited the fires deep inside.

"Yes, it is."

"So, we can start over? This can be our first date."

"I'd like that." I cleared my throat as a smile rushed to push my cheeks up nice and high. "Since it's our first date, I should let you know I have a six-year-old daughter who has hearing issues, and a nosy sister who lives with me, but who I love with all my heart." I beamed. "Oh, yeah, and a brother who will fight to protect me from anyone who will hurt me."

"Whew, I'm safe on that."

"How's that?"

"Because I will never hurt you."

My heart actually skipped a beat and tears welled in my eyes again. "And I make the same promise to you."

"So, we're doing this? We're going to start over and try again?"

"Nothing would please me more."

He leaned closer. "I should warn you though, I've been told I am a micromanager, but I am a damn good kisser."

I moved my lips to within inches of his face. "Prove it."

He brushed my hair away and cupped his hands around my cheeks. Pulling me close as he bridged the distance, he lightly brushed his lips over mine, teasing me with each ghostly caress. It was wild and intoxicating, and I wanted more, parting my lips just as he breezed over again. As we connected, the kiss turned more powerful, more possessive, and more sensual. I was putty in his capable hands, and if he was okay with all my baggage, then I was his for the taking as I couldn't wait to be a part of his world.

Epilogue

A month later…

David and I walked hand in hand down Main Street. The air had turned bitterly cold with the approaching winter, and we were huddled beneath our thick jackets, although it seemed to do little with the dampness hanging around.

We were just about at Sylvia's Bakery, one of our favourite places to have a sweet treat, when Libby burst through the door, mumbling, and waving her arms frantically.

I quickly looked at David but broke our connection as I stepped over to stop Libby. "What's going on?"

"He knows. He knows."

I put my arms on her shaking shoulders, and even though she wasn't wearing a jacket like she should've been, I knew she wasn't trembling from the cold.

"Libby," I stared into her eyes. "What happened?"

"He knows. He knows why I went after him. He feels

betrayed because he thinks I was just after my sister."

"Libby, honey, you need to slow down. You're not making any sense."

"He said it was over, that I used him to get to my sister." She avoided making eye contact but did manage to catch her breath. "And while it may be true, somewhere along the lines I fell in love with him, and it can't be over. I fell in love with him, can you believe it? But he just hung up on me and told me to beat it. But I love him so much." Like a caged animal, she was trying to free herself from my hold.

I swallowed down a pang of regret, for not having noticed she'd been falling in love. All this time, I thought she'd just been hanging out with the guy, having a little fun, and based on our conversations, that he was the one in deeper.

"I got to go. I need to try and make this right."

I stepped to the side, backing into David. "Go and do the right thing."

Libby started running.

Cupping my hands around my mouth, I yelled, "Tell him the truth. It always helps."

David wrapped his arms around me, whispering in my ear. "Yes, it does."

I melted into him; at the same time I twisted my head to gaze into his eyes. "For the rest of my life, I will never forgive myself for that."

"You should, I have. It's over and done with. You've made amends. It's time to let it go. There are other more important things to worry about." Tenderly, he tipped up my chin and planted a sweet kiss on my lips. "But I promise, all is good with me." He cocked his head as a shiver rippled through his body; his perfect, make me come hither body. "Come on, we're going to be late."

We walked into the heavily cinnamon-scented bakery and over to the table where my sister Mia sat with the love of her life, Zachary.

"God, Erin, every time I see you, you look all lit up inside." My sister beamed and jumped up to hug me. I swore, it never got old.

Zachary rose and also greeted me with a hug.

"Thanks," I said, tossing a grin toward David, who shook Zachary's hand. "I'm – we're – very happy. Vera is too."

"Sorry I'm late," Summer announced as she bounced into the bakery, and untying her scarf, flopped down in the seat next to me. "Your brother…" She flipped a stern expression to me and Mia. "Was being a major pain in the ass, and… well, I'm sorry. Did I miss anything?"

Mia shook her head. "We were just about to get started."

"Perfect." Summer leaned back against her chair.

"So the wedding date has been quietly announced, and there's a lot of hushed whispers as to the reason for such a rushed event."

"I think it's because she's pregnant." Summer had a smug little smile.

"Do you know something we don't?" I asked.

"No, I'm just saying, it sounds like it would be something fitting with both of their characters. They wouldn't want a baby without their union being official." She shrugged.

"People get married for other reasons other than pregnancy." I cocked my brow.

"Anyway." Mia cleared her throat. "Planning a wedding for six weeks from now doesn't give us a lot of time to work with." Mia opened her portfolio. "Zachary is scouting out last-minute reception locations, and I'm putting together places of interest for a photo shoot."

"That's great, but I'm not sure why I'm here? I have nothing to contribute to her wedding." I rested my hand on David's strong thigh and leaned back against his wall of chest.

As epic as the wedding was going to be, I had zero experience with it all. Summer and Adam weren't even close to thinking about marriage, Mia said she wanted to wait even though they'd been together for a couple of years, and Francesca? Hell would freeze over first, leaving me the next to possibly consider tying the knot, however, David and I hadn't yet discussed anything like that – it was way too soon, although, secretly, I had already said yes in my head.

How could I not? He was calm, organized, and enjoyed being around my daughter. Plus, he accepted me for all that I am. David made my heart soar, and in his presence, I felt a lightness I never knew I needed.

As corny as it sounded, he was the missing piece to my puzzle.

Summer leaned closer. "Amber wants you to design the centerpieces. She'll pay you, of course, but she really wants something amazing, and her first thought naturally was you."

"Me?" I pointed at my chest and blinked at the thought. "How many pieces are we talking about?"

Summer and Mia shared a smile; they clearly knew more than they were letting on. "Likely a dozen."

I exhaled, figuring it was going to be way more than that. After all, Amber was well known in this town and any wedding of hers would be a huge, spectacular affair.

"Well, that I can do. Wait, why isn't she here? Shouldn't I be discussing any ideas with her?"

"Since she's overseas for a while, she's put me in charge," Mia spoke and wiggled with radiance in her seat. "I've sort of become the makeshift wedding planner, since I know everyone and everything in this town inside out and backwards."

"Tell her the date so she can agree or disagree." Zachary nudged Mia. "She'll need time to create her art."

David and I leaned closer when Mia signaled us to. "The date hasn't been made public yet." She scanned the area to make sure we weren't being overheard and then dropped her voice to a barely audible level. "But she really wants an epic New Year's Eve wedding."

My eyes widened as I leaned back. "You're right, that doesn't give us a lot of time."

"It doesn't, but do you think you can do something wonderful?"

"Of course, she can." Both David and Summer answered at the same time.

The love of my life gazed into my eyes. "You work better under pressure."

"Maybe." I shifted in my seat, wondering if that's how he truly saw it.

"And don't forget about the Christmas market," Summer added. "That event will be even bigger."

Even bigger. Which reminded me of all the things I was working on for it – several layered ornaments, frames, door stackers. Now to add a dozen centerpieces to my list? Where was I going to conjure up the time?

Mia reached across the table. "Send me your ideas and the cost, and I'll have Amber approve it. She's got a pretty healthy budget."

No doubt. Marrying a rich European bazillionaire would give an endless bank account from which to draw funds from.

"Tell Amber I'd love to." I really couldn't say no. "I'll draw up some raw ideas and send them to her, or to you?"

"Email her, but let me know what she agrees to so we can work around that." Mia nodded and put a checkmark next to that item on her list. "Now, where do you think would be a great place for wedding photos?"

After throwing out some ideas and chatting for a little while longer, David and I were the first to leave and we walked back to my place.

"Do you think you'd design something for our wedding?" It was an innocent question to have asked, but it still revved up the butterflies in my stomach.

"Our wedding?"

"Yeah, someday. Would you want to make the decorations, or have someone else do it?"

I shrugged. "I don't know. Ask me again when the time comes."

When he didn't respond, I turned around, and there he was on bended knee.

No. No. NO!

This wasn't how I envisioned my only proposal to be. Although I hadn't given it a lot of thought, I didn't want it to be in front of Whimsical Whims.

He stood, giving me a quizzical look. "What? I was tying my shoe. What's with that look?"

I swallowed and stuttered, not sure how to answer. "I… um… well…"

His eyes widened. "Did you think I was? No way. It's too soon, right?"

"Right, *way* too soon." I gave him the side eye as he held my hand, and we resumed walking back to my house.

But when you know, you know, it's a feeling you can't shake away. It's that comfort in knowing how someone is imperfectly perfect for your life. That's how it was with David, and deep in my heart, he was the one I wanted to spend the rest of my life with.

My phone buzzed and I quickly retrieved it. *Libby.* I pushed the answer button after showing it to David. "What's up?"

"I can't find him, and I'm running out of options."

"Whoa – slow down." I pushed the speaker button after yanking the phone away from my ear.

"I can't." Her voice cut in and out. "I'm in love, and I have to tell him before I lose him forever. Help me, Erin. What do I have to do?"

David laughed beside me. "The smallest gestures have the biggest impact."

"Small gestures?"

I nodded, although she couldn't see that. "Offer to eat a chicken wrap. That'll seal the deal."

"That doesn't make any sense. Shit, I'm here. I gotta—"

"Libby?" I glanced at the display where the words 'call ended' appeared. "She hung up on me."

"Sealing the deal, eh?" There was an undeniable sparkle in his eyes as he licked his lips.

"Vera's home in an hour…"

I was already race-walking in that direction. We could be quick but tender, and the time crunch would most certainly add to the desire.

David grabbed my hand and pulled me off to the side.

"What are you doing? You're wasting time."

He ran his thumb down my cooled cheek, instantly warming it on contact. "Anytime spent with you is never wasted, my love."

I looked into his eyes. "You are seriously the sweetest. I love you."

"And I love you. And Vera. And your whole crazy connected family." His lips brushed over mine.

I pushed back into the kiss, ready to puddle right there against the brick wall. In a short time, David had become my everything, and I couldn't have been happier.

The Cheshire Bay Series

DREAMERS in CHESHIRE BAY

RETURN to CHESHIRE BAY

ADRIFT in CHESHIRE BAY

AWAKE in CHESHIRE BAY

CHRISTMAS in CHESHIRE BAY

JOURNEY to CHESHIRE BAY

CHARMED in CHESHIRE BAY

SECOND CHANCES in CHESHIRE BAY

UNFORGIVEN in CHESHIRE BAY

FLIRTY in CHESHIRE BAY

Dear Reader

This story gave me all the grey hairs. I'd written the story and hated it, so I rewrote most of it, and still hated it. I did this a few times over. I was so worried, especially with the preorder up, that I was not going to get it to a place where I actually liked the story before I needed to send it out to my trusted editor. I was worried sick. Then one night, in the wee hours when no one is awake and the house is quiet, something just clicked. And everything became crystal clear. Everything. When I got up in the morning, I sat and frantically typed. The words flowed. Nothing was fighting me anymore. It felt so good. And a few weeks later, as I reread it, I finally loved the story. Yep, it actually took that many drafts. These two were so complicated, more so than Summer & Adam, but it makes sense now why – with Adam and Erin related, naturally they're going to have that same fight back instinct. Ha-hah.

After sending the story out to beta readers, they really helped polish it, and relief settled in. I made the editor deadline (with time to spare) and alleviated *that* worry. Now, time to stress about how you, the reader, enjoyed the story.

By the way, did you learn a few signs? As an insight, my youngest child did not speak until he was three (he could hear, just couldn't talk). There was no mama, no dada at the suggested age, and after some time of encouraging him to 'use his words', it still didn't happen, so ASL became a godsend to us, and it totally changed his (and our) world. Finally, our child could communicate with us (and others as we translated), and we had a happy child again. It was life changing. By the time my son started school, we had officially added ASL to our learned languages (bringing it to three; English, French, and ASL). I'd always wanted to incorporate this into one of my stories, and Vera was the perfect child, so hopefully you learned a sign or two. It's just a beautiful language, and although we don't use it as much, we were grateful to have learned it.

As always, thank you so much for spending your valuable time with me. You have no idea how much I appreciate you for doing that.

Much love,

H.M. Shander

acknowledgements

First – my Shander family, whom you may know on my social media platforms as Hubs, The Teen, and Little Dude.

To my parents and in-laws and extended family –

To my beta readers – Kim B, Alicia D, and Jessica H. My goodness. You each brought something unique to the table and helped polish this story. I loved the comments where you laughed out loud, or gasped, or the inquisitive thoughts of why a character was acting in a way that seemed out of character. You were my Erin's, calling me out on some scenes, and I'm forever grateful! Because of your feedback, the story is better, tighter, and filled with more emotion. THANK YOU!

To my cover designer – Eleanor. The moment I saw these two, I just knew they were Erin & David. That's exactly how I'd pictured them in my mind. It was like they were meant to be on the cover, and you knew exactly how to bring them to perfection. And yes, I agree, we are running out of colours to use. Good thing this is the second last book in the series. (Okay, now I'm crying…) But you know I'll be back for more. You're worth every penny!

To my editor – Irina. Got this one to you early. Woohoo! Thank you for your insight, for finding that little tiny plot hole and highlighting it. How many passes did I do and I still missed that? Sheesh. I know you're moving on to bigger and better things, but I'll still be here righting the wrong werds, so know that you are still desperately needed. LOL.

If I missed you, it certainly wasn't intentional. I know I couldn't be where I am without the help of so many others. Thank you! And thank you for reading and making it all the way to the end. You all rock.

about the author

USA TODAY bestselling author H.M. Shander is a stargazing, romantic at heart who once attended Space Camp and wanted to pilot the space shuttle, not just any STS – specifically Columbia. However, the only shuttle she operates in her real world is the #momtaxi; a speedy electric car that zooms her two kids to school, work, and whatever sporting event or activity they are currently involved with. When she's not commandeering Elektra, you can find the elementary school librarian surrounded by classes of children as she reads the best storybooks in multiple voices. After she's tucked her endearing kids into bed and kissed her trophy husband goodnight, she moonlights as a contemporary romance novelist; the writer of sassy heroines and sweet, swoon-worthy heroes who find love in the darkest of places.

For all the latest release news, subscribe to H.M. Shander's newsletter, or you can follow her on Twitter(@HM_Shander), Facebook (hmshander), Instagram (@hmshander) or check out her website at www.hmshander.com.

Thanks for reading– all the way to the very end. I'm grateful you're here.

www.ingramcontent.com/pod-product-compliance
Lightning Source LLC
Chambersburg PA
CBHW050418260626
47156CB00003B/1063

9781990240201